STORM RUNNERS

ROLAND SMITH

SCHOLASTIC PRESS
NEW YORK

Text copyright © 2011 by Roland Smith

Library of Congress Cataloging-in-Publication Data

Smith, Roland, 1951-
Storm runners / Roland Smith. — 1st ed. p. cm.
Summary: Twelve-year-old Chase Masters travels the country with his father,
a "storm runner," but he is tested in ways he never could have imagined when he
and a new friend are caught in a hurricane near St. Petersburg, Florida.

[1. Hurricanes—Fiction. 2. Storm chasers—Fiction. 3. Conduct of life—Fiction.
4. Fathers and sons—Fiction. 5. Circus animals—Fiction. 6. Saint Petersburg
(Fla.)—Fiction.] I. Title.

PZ7.S65766Sto 2011
[Fic]—dc22
2010032720

ISBN 978-0-545-08175-7

10 9 8 7 6 5 4 3 2 1   11 12 13 14 15

Printed in the U.S.A.   23

First edition, March 2011

Book design by Phil Falco

DISCARD
FOR NIKI

ONE YEAR EARLIER...

Chase Masters decided it was time to repair the tree house in the backyard. It had been his little sister Monica's favorite place. She'd spent so much time up there they'd nicknamed her Little Monkey — a nickname Monica had liked.

He started by tearing out a couple of rotted support beams and replacing them with treated four-by-sixes. He was going to fix the roof next, but he never got to it.

The next morning, he and his father, John, were sitting in the kitchen, eating breakfast. Eggs, pancakes, bacon — a Sunday tradition since Chase had been born.

"Want some more grub, Chase?" his father asked.

Chase shook his head. He'd already eaten five eggs and a half dozen strips of bacon, and he was still working on a stack of pancakes tall enough to sit on.

His father poured himself another cup of black coffee, sat down at the table, and looked out the back window.

"Thunderstorm," he said. "After we clean up I better head out to the jobsite and double-check to make sure everything's tied down and covered. Want to come?"

"Sure."

Large raindrops began to splatter the backyard.

Chase's father leaned closer to the window. "Are those tools lying outside?"

What his father was really asking was, "Why in the BLANK did you leave those tools outside?"

Tools were like religious artifacts in the Masters house. After each use, they were to be cleaned, oiled if necessary, and put away in their proper place — and each tool had only one proper place.

"Sorry." Chase jumped up from the table.

"Relax. I'll get 'em. Finish your pancakes. It'll give me a chance to see what kind of job you did on those supports."

"I did it right."

Chase's father grinned. "I have no doubt. You were trained by the Master."

Chase returned the grin. And it wasn't because of his father's terrible pun. Chase was relieved that his father wasn't upset that he was fixing the tree house.

When Monica was five years old she'd wandered off, sending the whole family into a terrified panic. They had searched for hours. Chase's mother had called the police. They were about ready to issue an AMBER Alert when Chase found Monica sound asleep in the old oak tree in the backyard. If she had rolled over, she would have fallen twenty-five feet. Chase and his father (mostly his father) had started building the tree house the next morning. Soon Monica was spending almost as much time up in the tree house as she was in their real house.

The tree house had been sitting empty for a little over a year now, and Chase had not mentioned his repair plans to his father. There was an unspoken rule in the Masters household: The deaths of his mother and sister were not to be talked about, because the subject opened sores that hurt for days.

As far as Chase knew, his father hadn't set foot in Monica's bedroom since the accident. It was almost as if he thought she was still in there and would come running out one day, filling the house with her wild, uninhibited giggling. Chase would have given almost anything to hear that laugh again.

Chase watched his father walk across the yard in the now pouring rain. John Masters hadn't bothered to put on a coat and he was getting drenched. His lightweight cowboy shirt clung to his lean, ropy muscles. His brown hair had turned black in the torrent. He climbed the slick rungs screwed into the gnarled trunk and inspected Chase's work as if he were a structural engineer, which he wasn't. He was a builder. One of the best in the city. He had built their house, and several other houses in the neighborhood too. After he'd married Chase's mother, he'd started a construction company with her brother, Bob.

Chase's father climbed down from the tree and gave his son a thumbs-up sign, which Chase took to mean that he could continue with his renovation and maybe, just maybe, they could put the past behind them and get on with their lives.

It turned out that they did get on with their lives, but it wasn't the life Chase had been expecting.

Chase's father reached down and picked up the nail gun. He shook the rain off of it, looked up at the sky . . .

Chase was still a little shaky about what happened next.

There was a blinding flash of white light followed by a deafening explosion that shook the house. When Chase's eyes cleared from the flash, he saw his father crumpled beneath the tree. His clothes were smoking. Chase ran out of the house, yelling. The sharp stench of ozone filled the backyard. His father wasn't breathing. The snaps on his shirt were fused to his chest. People showed up from all over the neighborhood. A couple of them were doctors. They started giving him CPR.

Chase couldn't watch.

He looked up at the tree.

His father's left boot was dangling by its shoelace from a lower branch.

Two days later his father came out of his coma.

When Chase told him how terrible he felt about leaving the tools outside, his father laughed and said, "That bolt of lighting was waiting for me my whole life, Chase. If it hadn't nailed me in the backyard, it would have gotten me in the front yard, walking to my truck, or later at the jobsite. You can't hide from your fate."

On the road with his father over the past year, Chase had thought a lot about the word fate *and decided that it was one of those little words with a big meaning. . . .*

01:58 PM

When my father got struck by lightning, so did I, Chase thought. *When Mom and Monica died, so did I . . . a little. . . .*

"I guess you can't separate your fate from those you're with," Chase said quietly.

"What?" his father asked.

Chase jumped. He hadn't meant to say that last part out loud. "Nothing . . . uh . . . just thinking about a song."

"You want the radio on?"

"No, I'm fine."

Chase and his father were in Florida speeding down a road along the Gulf of Mexico. Chase's father had one hand on the steering wheel of their 4x4 truck. In his other he held a travel mug of black coffee. Chase's job was to replenish the mug from the Thermos at his feet, which he had filled four hours earlier in the weather-battered fifth-wheel trailer they were pulling. His father called the fifth-wheel the Shack. It was where they lived. It was nicer on the inside than the outside. The rough exterior was the result of a hailstorm in Oklahoma two weeks ago. Chase had been inside the Shack when it hit. The worst part had been the sound. His ears had rung for twenty-four hours after the ten-minute pounding. When he'd opened the door, the ground had been covered in golf-ball-size ice pellets for as far as he could see. A mile away a farmer had been killed running from his John Deere combine to his house. He should have stayed inside the combine.

"What time is it?" his father asked.

His father did not wear a watch. The perfectly running clock on the dash had been covered with black electrical tape. At the top of almost every hour (when they were together) he would ask Chase, who wore a radio-controlled atomic-time watch, that same question.

"Two o'clock," Chase said. "Exactly."

"Perfect."

The Internal Clock Game. This was just one of the games his father played during their frequent long drives. Another game was How to Get Out of Doom City. This consisted of his father picking a random street in a random city, and a disaster like a flood. The goal was for Chase to quickly find high ground, then plot a route that would get him out of town before the disaster caught up with him.

Chase wondered if Tomás played driving games. He doubted it. Tomás was behind them, driving the Shop — a forty-foot trailer pulled by a Mack semi tractor — by himself. Tomás's living quarters were in the front part of the trailer, with a separate entrance. The rest was filled with two dirt bikes, an all-terrain quad, and enough tools and supplies to build a three-story home. Behind the Shop, Tomás was pulling a second 4x4 truck.

Signs on the sides of all the rigs read, M.D. EMERGENCY SERVICES, followed by a 1-800 number.

Obviously the *M.D.* didn't stand for *Medical Doctor*, but sometimes the authorities thought it did and Chase's father didn't correct them. *M.D.* stood for *Masters of Disaster*. In his father's world, everything had a double meaning.

About a week after the lightning strike, the economy was struck by recession. The building industry tanked. Chase's father and uncle's business was on the verge of bankruptcy. Uncle Bob was on the verge of an emotional collapse.

Chase's father wasn't worried at all. He had other plans. He sold everything they owned, including their house and their vacation cabin on Mount Hood. With the proceeds, he bought the Shack and the Shop, paid off his half of the construction company's debts, then signed the company over to a grateful but stunned Uncle Bob. . . .

"What are you going to do, John?"

"Start over. See the country."

"What about Chase?"

"He'll go with me, of course."

"What about school?"

"He'll go to school."

Chase had been to three schools in the past year and was heading toward his fourth, provided it wasn't wiped off the face of the earth by Hurricane Emily, who was whirling her way counterclockwise across the Gulf of Mexico.

Emily had started out a few weeks earlier as an innocent little thunderstorm in Ethiopia. She moved west over the Sahara Desert, picking up sand and heat, then swept out into the Atlantic, where she became a tropical storm and got her name. As the trade winds pushed her farther west she gathered humidity and power. At seventy-four miles an hour she graduated from a tropical storm to a hurricane.

Which is more than I'm going to do if we don't settle down in a school for more than two months, Chase thought.

He had just gotten used to the school in Oklahoma when his father pulled the plug and started them toward Emily. Coincidentally, or maybe not, Emily was his mother's first name. His father still had work when they'd left Oklahoma. Chase wondered if the hurricane's name had anything to do with their leaving so quickly, but he knew better than to ask. Nothing could shift his father's mood faster than bringing up his mom or sister.

Chase looked over at his father. He used to know him face-on. Now he knew him mostly in profile from the passenger seat. About the only time they were together anymore was in the truck driving to a disaster. When his father and Tomás were working, they slept in hotels, only coming back to the Shack & Shop to pick up supplies. Chase had thought that being on the road would bring him and his father closer together. In some ways it had, but right now, sitting three feet apart, they might as well have been in different solar systems.

Chase's relationship with Tomás was not much better, but theirs was a language problem. Tomás's English wasn't good and Chase's Spanish was nonexistent. Chase wasn't sure how Tomás and his father communicated so well. A combination of Spanglish and telepathy, he guessed. Tomás had worked for Chase's father for more than twenty years. When his father told Uncle Bob that he was taking Tomás with them, Uncle Bob almost wept.

"I'll have to hire three new guys to replace him," Uncle Bob had said.

"Four," his father had replied.

More like five, in Chase's opinion. Tomás was at least ten years older than his father, but he was a building machine. Tomás never walked between tasks. He jogged, like everything was an emergency. A few years before they hit the road, Uncle Bob had jokingly said that he would give Tomás a five-grand cash bonus if he could frame a two-story house that passed building inspection in twenty-four hours. Tomás did it in twenty-two. The building inspector said it was the best framing job he'd ever seen. Uncle Bob handed over the cash.

Tomás was married and had eight kids, but Chase had never met his wife, or the rest of his family. Neither had his father. They lived someplace in Mexico. Tomás visited them once a year around Christmas, and Chase assumed he sent most of his money down south to them. In his truck he kept laminated photos of all of the kids arranged by age. On top of his dash was a plastic statue of Saint Christopher, patron saint of travelers. Saint Christopher was also invoked against lightning. Tomás had given his father a Saint Christopher's medal when he was in the hospital. So far, it had worked.

On most Sundays, Tomás put his hammer down for a few hours and went to church. Chase had gone with him a couple of times. He didn't think Tomás understood a word the priest was saying, but that wasn't the point.

Chase believed that Tomás went to church for the same reason he had left everything behind to join Chase's father.

Tomás was loyal.

02:16 PM

They had left the freeway and were now driving down a two-lane road. Tomás had taken the lead, which was unusual because as far as Chase knew, Tomás had never been to Florida.

They always parked the Shack & Shop on private property — high ground — at least forty miles from where his father thought he and Tomás would be working. *Thought* because they didn't really know where they'd find work. That depended on where the storm hit and the amount of damage it caused — two things nobody could predict. But Chase's father was pretty good at guessing.

As with the Internal Clock Game, Chase was not sure how his father did this. Before the lightning strike, his father hadn't been at all interested in weather. After he got out of the hospital, he had the Weather Channel on twenty-four hours a day. He read every book about weather he could get his hands on. He bought weather software for his laptop. After two weeks he could predict the weather anywhere, almost perfectly, several days out. Chase joked that he should become a meteorologist for a local television station. His father told him he had something very different in mind.

Another thing that changed after the lightning strike was his father's sleeping pattern. He'd always been an eight-hours-a-night guy. On weekends he'd sleep nine or ten hours if he could get away with it. Not anymore. His father hadn't slept more than four hours a night since the strike and he never seemed to get tired. Chase thought he had more energy now than he did before the strike. It was almost as if his father had electricity in his veins instead of blood.

02:31 PM

Tomás stopped the semi in front of a chain-link gate. He jumped out, swung the double gate open, then jogged back to the cab. Chase wondered if maybe Tomás had lightning in his body too.

They followed Tomás through. Chase got out and closed the gate behind them, then climbed back into the cab.

"What is this place?"

"A farm," his father answered. "Tomás's brother, Arturo, works here."

Chase didn't know Tomás had a brother.

"They need some minor repairs," his father continued. "I told them that we'd fix 'em up if they let us park here for free. You're in charge of the repairs. Tomás and I will be in Saint Petersburg — Saint Pete, as they call it."

Chase hoped his father was right about the repairs being minor.

"Where's the school?"

"About ten miles away. You'll have to drive the quad down to the road to catch the bus."

"You think the storm is going to hit up here?"

"I haven't checked the satellite images since early this morning, but there's a chance it could shift northeast. Palm Breeze might get nicked, but you'll be okay. This is the highest ground in the county. You'll still need to be alert, though. You know the routine."

Chase did know the routine. Sitting at his feet, next to the Thermos, was his go bag — a daypack that each of them had within reach twenty-four hours a day. Inside was everything they needed to survive for three days: satellite phone (for when the landlines and cell signals failed), first aid kit, rain gear, bottled water, camp stove, flares, freeze-dried food, energy bars, knife, butane lighter, binoculars, and several other items — none of which they'd had to use . . . yet.

The farm wasn't like any farm Chase had seen before. The fences were made out of heavy-duty chain link. About every twenty feet there was a warning: DANGER! ELECTRIFIED!

Electrified against what? Chase thought. *We've gone half a mile and I haven't seen a single animal.*

They came to a second gate. On the other side were four large metal buildings. They pulled the rigs through the gate, parked, and stepped out into the humid air.

A man came out of the building directly in front of them. He was small. Very small. He pulled off his leather gloves as he walked toward them.

"You're Mr. Masters?"

"John," his father said, holding out his hand. "This is Tomás. And this is my son, Chase."

Chase shook the man's little hand. The man stared at

him with bright blue eyes. "You're probably wondering what to call me."

"What do you mean?"

"Midget, dwarf," the man said. "I don't mind any of them, but *dwarf* is the appropriate word since I have dwarfism. But the acceptable term if you want to be politically correct is *little person*." He patted his head. "L.P. for short."

He laughed at his own joke. Chase and his father smiled. Tomás smiled too, but Chase doubted he had gotten the pun.

"My name's Marco Rossi," the man said. "I'm pleased to meet all of you." He looked at Tomás. "I'm afraid your brother, Arturo, isn't here. He and the others took off yesterday with a load of animals, but you're still welcome. In fact, I'm glad to have you. We're a little shorthanded."

"Actually, Tomás and I won't be around much," Chase's father explained. "We need to head to Saint Pete and help prepare for the storm, but Chase will be staying here, and he's pretty handy."

"That'll increase our manpower by a third, so I'm grateful. Do you like animals, Chase?"

"Sure, but I don't know much about cows and horses."

Chase didn't know much about cats and dogs, either. His mother had been allergic to them, so they'd never had any at the house.

Marco laughed. "You don't need to know much about cows and horses on this farm." He looked at the rigs. "What happened to the fifth-wheel?"

"Hailstorm in Oklahoma."

"Hope that doesn't happen here."

"Hurricanes are too warm to produce hail," Chase's father pointed out. "Tornadoes are a different story. Twisters and hail go together. The problems with hurricanes are wind, rain, and storm surge." He looked at Chase. "Ten to three?"

Chase nodded, though his father was three seconds fast.

"We better get moving. I want to be in Saint Pete before it shuts down for the night."

Tomás jogged over to the semi and fired it up.

Within twenty minutes, Tomás and Chase's father had parked the rigs in one of the buildings, loaded their 4x4s with supplies, and were on their way to Saint Petersburg.

Chase spent the next hour setting up the Shack & Shop.

The building was perfect. Concrete floor. Steel struts covered by heavy-gauge aluminum panels. Plenty of electrical receptacles to plug in to. Water. Septic system. The only problem was the heat. It was like the inside of a barbeque. Chase turned up the AC in the fifth-wheel and left. It wasn't much better outside, but the light breeze dried the sweat on his face and T-shirt.

After they parked, Marco had needed to hurry off and take care of something. He told Chase to find him somewhere on the grounds when he finished. Chase walked over to the nearest building and opened the door, expecting to see a little person. What he found instead was a girl about his age, his height, feeding a giraffe.

She was wearing shorts and a T-shirt. Her long black hair was wet and combed straight back as if she'd just stepped out of the shower.

"Hi. Dad said you'd be by. I'm Nicole Rossi."

She looked at Chase for a moment, then started laughing.

"What's so funny?"

"The look on your face. Are you surprised to see a giraffe, or are you surprised that I'm Marco Rossi's daughter?"

Chase smiled sheepishly. "Both, I guess."

"Little people can have regular-size children. My older sister is little. My older brother is big. Huge, in fact. He's a defensive tackle for the Georgia Bulldogs. And if you're wondering why my hair is wet, I just finished swimming laps."

"You have a pool?"

"Almost everyone in Florida has a pool, or a neighbor who has a pool you can use. If we didn't have free access to pools, we would melt in the summer."

The giraffe bent its knobby head down and wrapped a purplish tongue around the carrot Nicole was holding.

At that exact same moment, there was a terrifying roar that shook the metal building and reverberated inside Chase's chest and all the way down to his toes. He'd never heard — or *felt* — anything like that in his life.

"Nothing to be afraid of. That's just Simba, one of our lions. He's in a cage."

"You have lions in here?"

"A bunch of them."

"What *is* this place?"

"Winter quarters for the Rossi Brothers' Circus. My dad didn't tell you?"

"Winter quarters?"

"You don't know much about circuses."

"I don't know *anything* about circuses."

"Circuses are seasonal, especially for tent shows like ours. We can't put up the big top or get where we're going if it's snowing. We need a place to keep the animals during the winter. The whole show should be back here by now, but we picked up a couple extra months in Mexico. It's just as well because of the storm. Arturo and our winter quarters crew are hauling animals south of the border."

"Not the giraffe."

"Gertrude," Nicole said. "She'd stand over twenty feet on a lowboy semitrailer. Too tall to fit under overpasses. She was only on the show for a couple of years when she was a baby. Now she's a full-time resident here."

"Like you and your dad?"

"That's right. Someone has to be here to take care of the surplus animals and run the farm. And I have school. My mother and sister are on the road with the show, along with my two uncles. Sometimes we catch up with the show for a few days during the summer if I have a swim meet close by."

"So, you compete."

Nicole shrugged. "I can tread water."

Chase was going to ask if her mother was a little person too, but the question was blown out of his thoughts by another chest-rattling roar.

"Come on. I'll take you over to meet the pride."

04:12 PM

Simba was as big as his roar. He rubbed his thick black mane back and forth along the chain-link holding area with such force Chase was afraid the wire was going to snap. Nicole didn't seem the least bit concerned. She put her fingers through the links and scratched Simba under the chin.

"Simba's thirteen. He was born the same year I was."

Which means we're the same age, Chase thought. "Why isn't Simba with the show?"

"He mauled our trainer a couple of years ago."

Chase took a small step backward, which he hoped Nicole hadn't noticed. "How badly?"

"It could have been worse." Nicole continued scratching Simba's chin. "The trainer could have been killed and Simba might have been shot. The trainer was in the hospital for two weeks. We decided it was time for Simba to retire. But I think he misses the road."

"What about the trainer?"

"He's back with the show. Getting mauled is no big deal."

"Unless you're the one getting mauled."

"I suppose that's true," Nicole agreed. "But most cat trainers will tell you that getting mauled is not a matter of *if*. It's a matter of *when* and how bad the mauling is going to be."

Nicole led him outside the building to an attached enclosure with four more lions. "Three lionesses and one lion." She pointed. "You can see the male's just starting to get his mane."

He was about half the size of Simba. "Will he be in the show someday?"

"Maybe. He was someone's idea of a wonderful pet. The state confiscated him. He was starving when they brought him in. We take in a lot of animals like that. I think there are as many exotic animals in private hands in Florida as there are pools. We get the animals back on their feet and give them to rehabilitation facilities or zoos. Sometimes we put them in the show, but not very often. Not all animals are cut out for the circus . . . not all people are either."

"How about you?"

Nicole laughed. "Oh, I think it's a foregone conclusion that I'll be in the circus when I grow up. That is, if there are circuses. They aren't as popular as they used to be. A lot of them have folded. One way or the other, I'll be working with animals. If the circus dies, I'm going to be a marine mammal veterinarian. What about you, Chase Masters?" She turned her beautiful brown eyes on him. "What are you going to be when you grow up?"

Chase had spent a lot of time thinking about this. Like his father, he was good with his hands. He enjoyed building and fixing things, but he wasn't sure he wanted to become a contractor or a builder.

"I'm not sure," he said. "Maybe I'll become a lion tamer."

"Funny."

"Why isn't Simba out here with the other lions?"

"He doesn't get along with them. We alternate him outside by himself every other day."

Nicole led Chase over to another building. Inside was a leopard named Hector.

"Odd name," Chase said.

"Odd cat. We didn't name him. He was confiscated from a drug runner."

Hector was a third of Simba's size, but for some reason he looked a lot more lethal. He paced back and forth restlessly.

"You don't want to get too close to Hector," Nicole said. "He's very aggressive and fast as lightning. I'm surprised the drug runner who owned him lived long enough to get arrested."

"What are you going to do with him?"

"He's not going on the show, that's for sure. Dad has a couple of zoos that are interested. He'll be leaving the farm soon, but that won't be soon enough for me. Old Hector is as bright as he is fast. Getting him into the holding area so we can clean his cage is a major ordeal. About half the time, he gets in and out of the holding area with the meat we bait him *in* with before we can even close the door. He figured out that he could get a double portion that way on his first day here."

"He doesn't look fat," Chase said.

"He's not. He burns calories pacing and lunging at us when we get within range of his claws."

In the cage next to Hector's, an ancient brown bear slept curled in a corner. Across from the cages were two large stalls. Three zebras stood together in one, and the other held four ostriches. At the far end of the building was an indoor/outdoor aviary filled with colorful parrots.

As strange and wonderful as the animals were, the thing that was beginning to interest Chase the most was his tour guide. He was looking forward to staying on the farm, learning about circuses . . . and Nicole.

"Do you let people come up here to see the animals?" he asked.

"Friends," she said. "We try to keep a low profile. We're not really set up for visitors. But that might change with the baby elephant."

"You have a baby elephant?"

"Almost."

"What do you mean?"

Instead of answering, Nicole led him to the only building they hadn't been in, which was by far the largest. The three other buildings would have all easily fit inside.

"This is where we rehearse the acts and train the animals during the winter. And that's the bunkhouse for the roughnecks." She pointed to a smaller attached building to the right.

"What's a roughneck?"

"They drive the trucks; put up the big top; set up the rings, cages, apparatus; assist the animal trainers and performers. Without them, there wouldn't be a show. Arturo is a roughneck, but he doesn't live in the bunkhouse. He's been with the circus for nearly thirty years and pretty much runs the farm now. He has a house on the property. The bunkhouse is empty at the moment, except for my dad. He's been sleeping down here for a couple of weeks."

"Why?"

"I'll show you."

Nicole opened the door.

The building was lit with bright spotlights hanging from the ceiling, shining down on three large circus rings. The ring closest to them had a steel cage in the center, which Chase assumed was for the big cats. The middle ring had a huge safety net stretched across it. Hanging above the net was a tightwire and an array of trapeze equipment. Marco Rossi was in the third ring, hosing down an elephant and scrubbing her wrinkled gray skin with a long-handled deck brush.

"How's it going, Dad?" Nicole said.

"I should have gotten AC in here years ago," he said. "It's like a furnace!"

"We could open the doors on either end."

"Right, and Pet will pull her leg off trying to get outside."

Chase noticed the elephant had chains around her left front foot and right rear foot. "Why's she chained?"

"So she doesn't float to the ceiling," Nicole and Marco said in unison, then started laughing.

"Sorry, Chase," Marco said. "Old circus joke. Can't help ourselves. On the show, people ask that question a thousand times a day. Elephants are chained to a picket line so they don't run off — or whack somebody." He handed the hose and brush to Nicole and stepped out of the ring.

"In the case of Pet here, we have her chained up so she doesn't dismantle the building. We don't have an elephant-proof building on the farm. The elephants we use on our show winter in Texas. Our elephant guy has a good setup down there. And Pet would be there right now, but she's twenty-two months pregnant and we didn't want to risk trucking her that far so close to term. Elephant births in captivity are rare. We've never had one in the hundred years our circus has been on the road. So, as you might imagine, we're pretty excited. . . ."

"And nervous," Nicole added, shooting a stream of water into Pet's open mouth.

"I'll admit it," Marco said. "I am nervous. What if something goes wrong? Our vet doesn't know anything about elephant births."

"Not many vets do," Nicole said.

"There's a doc on the West Coast who's seen dozens of elephants born. I've been on the phone with him every day, offered him a fortune to fly out here and supervise the birth, but he said it would be a waste of money. He told me that Pet will have her calf when she has it. She'll take care of it or she won't. It'll be healthy or unhealthy. He'll come out after it's born if there's a problem."

"When's the baby due?"

"Anytime now. We're not exactly sure when she was bred. As elephants go, Pet's pretty steady, but the past few days she's been acting up. She can't seem to get comfortable when she lies down, she's off her feed, and yesterday she took a poke at me with her trunk for no good reason, which is really out of character for her. Normally she's the most easygoing elephant I've ever been around."

Nicole turned the hose off, wound it up out of Pet's reach, then joined them.

"Your grandmother is looking for you," Marco said. "She said something about you not finishing your laps."

"I finished most of them," Nicole said. "I came down to help. You can't take care of everything here, especially with an elephant calf on its way."

"I managed to take care of the farm long before you were born," Marco reminded her. "Your grandmother also said that she needs help with her boxes, and mentioned something about sweet potato pie."

Nicole smiled. "I'll go."

"Take Chase with you. She's probably already mad at you for not taking him to the house to introduce him."

"You didn't take him up there either," Nicole teased.

"I have pachyderm problems. What's your excuse?"

"We better go," Nicole said.

They left Marco and Pet, and started up a long, twisting driveway to a farmhouse overlooking the enclosures and buildings.

"Are there any other animals on the farm?" Chase asked.

"Aside from Momma Rossi's squirrel monkey, Poco, no."

"Who's Momma Rossi?"

"My grandmother. She's up at the house, packing."

"Where's she going?"

"She thinks the hurricane is going to hit the house."

"My dad's pretty good at predicting the weather. He says it's going to make landfall south of here. Probably around Saint Pete."

"Momma Rossi is rarely wrong," Nicole said. "She can see the future . . . and sometimes even the past."

05:02 PM

Chase followed Nicole onto the screened porch of the Rossis' old farmhouse. He looked at the sofas and chairs scattered about and wondered what it would be like to sit there in the evening, listening to lion tamers, clowns, acrobats, and little people talking about their day.

To get through the front door, they had to move several boxes of framed newspaper articles, photos, and other circus memorabilia to the side.

"Where's she moving this stuff?"

"We have a waterproof storage container out back by the pool."

Nicole led the way into a large kitchen, where the counters, cupboards, and appliances were at least two feet lower than they'd normally be. Momma Rossi, gray-haired and a bit shorter than her son, stood at the sink peeling sweet potatoes. Sitting next to the sink was a small green monkey wearing a diaper. He was holding a potato peel in one hand and scratching his leg with the other. Momma Rossi turned around and gave them a bright smile.

She put her hand out. "You must be Chase Masters. Welcome to our home."

"Thank you." Chase took her hand.

Momma Rossi stared at him with dark eyes and her smile faded.

"I'm so sorry about your mother and sister."

Chase froze.

"What are you talking about?" Nicole asked.

Momma Rossi gripped Chase's hand more tightly. "A car accident on a mountain. I'm sure it hasn't been easy for you or your father."

Tomás must have told Arturo, Chase thought. But looking into Momma Rossi's dark eyes, he had an eerie feeling that wasn't how she knew. . . .

TWO YEARS EARLIER...

It had rained every day Chase had been at Boy Scout camp, and it was still raining. He was standing in the parking lot with his troop leader, Mr. Murphy. All morning, one by one, parents had been picking up their drenched Scouts. Now it was just Chase and Mr. Murphy.

Mr. Murphy looked at his watch for the hundredth time. "Are you sure your parents were clear on when and where to pick you up?"

"Yes, sir. Like I told you, I talked to them last night. Mom said that they were driving up with my little sister. On the way

home we're going to stop at our cabin and pick up a load of fire-wood for the house."

"Maybe they stopped at the cabin first."

"I don't think so. Dad wouldn't haul a truckload of wood all the way up here, then drive it back down the mountain."

"You're probably right. Do you have a phone at your cabin?"

"No."

Mr. Murphy pulled his cell out and called Chase's house and his parents' cells again. All three calls went to voice mail.

Chase was starting to feel sick. His parents were never late for anything.

"We can't stand here all day waiting," Mr. Murphy said. "How about if I leave a note for them here and voice mails on their phones saying I've taken you to my house?"

"Okay."

Chase tossed his soggy gear into the back of Mr. Murphy's SUV.

About halfway down the mountain, they ran into a terrible traffic jam. Chase was so worried about his parents not showing up that he barely noticed the line of cars stretching ahead of them . . . until they reached the end of it. On the opposite side of the highway, at least a half dozen police cars with flashing lights clustered on the shoulder. A tow truck was winching a blue SUV out of the ditch.

"That's my parents' car!" Chase shouted.

"Are you still a Boy Scout?" Momma Rossi asked.

"What?" Chase pulled his hand away from Momma Rossi quickly.

"Are you okay?" Nicole asked.

"Yeah, I just . . . uh . . ."

"I asked if you were still a Boy Scout," Momma Rossi repeated.

"No, we've been traveling," he said.

"Helping people," Momma Rossi said.

Chase nodded, but he knew it wasn't exactly true. . . .

At that moment, John Masters and Tomás were trolling separate parts of Saint Petersburg. John was driving through the business district. Tomás was driving through the wealthier residential areas.

If a business or home owner — never a contractor — was out making preparations for the storm, they'd stop, introduce themselves, then offer to give them a hand . . . for free. Tomás's poor English was not a hindrance. His skilled hands transcended all language barriers.

Both men knew precisely how to prepare a home or business for disaster. They were fast and efficient. They also knew that if the wind was strong enough, no preparation was going to save an expensive building or home from damage.

The grateful owner usually tried to pay them for their time, but they refused. Instead they handed over a couple of M.D. Emergency Services business cards and told the owners to call if they had any problems.

If the winds were strong enough, and the water high enough, they would all have problems, and they would call. But the second round of repairs wouldn't be free.

05:07 PM

Nicole picked up a paring knife from the counter. "I suppose you want some help peeling sweet potatoes."

"Since they're your sweet potatoes," Momma Rossi said, "you're darned right I want help. And what about your laps?" She put her hands on her hips and tried to look mad, but there was a sparkle in her eyes. "You did about half of what you were supposed to do."

"I did enough. The meet is in three days. I don't want to wear myself out before the competition. I was feeding Gertrude and the cats so Dad didn't have to."

"All right," Momma Rossi said. "Because we have a guest, and because we have a lot to do, I'll let it go this time."

"Scoot, peel thief!" Nicole said. Poco grabbed another potato peel, climbed to the top of the refrigerator, and glared down at her.

"Make yourself at home," Momma Rossi said to Chase. "This could take a while. Nicole is a very fast swimmer but a very slow potato peeler."

"Very funny, Momma."

"I can move those boxes if you want," Chase offered.

"That would be nice," Momma Rossi said. "But it might not be as easy as you think. For one thing, I'm not certain there's room in the container. Marco and Nicole haven't done a very good job of packing. The boxes need to be reorganized and restacked."

"No problem." After a year of Shack & Shop duty, Chase was an expert organizer.

Nicole put the knife down. "Since you're blaming me for the mess, maybe I better give him a hand."

"I think Chase is more than capable of hauling and organizing boxes on his own. And I need you to make the sweet potato pie . . . unless you'd prefer for Chase to eat my version."

Nicole laughed. "I guess that wouldn't be polite to our guest."

Momma Rossi snapped a towel at her playfully.

"I'm not exactly your guest," Chase said. It wasn't a rule, but they didn't usually hang out with the people who owned the property they parked on. "We have everything we need in the fifth-wheel. You don't need to feed me."

"Nonsense," Momma Rossi said. "I don't know how to cook for less than a dozen people, and with you, there are only four of us tonight."

"I wouldn't argue with Momma Rossi," Nicole said. "Dad tried to talk her out of getting the container. Guess who won?"

"He'll be happy our things are safe. Do you like sweet potato pie, Chase?"

"I like pie and I like sweet potatoes, but I've never had them together."

"You haven't lived until you've eaten Nicole's sweet potato pie."

Chase carried two boxes past a large modern pool, which did not fit with the old two-story farmhouse. The Rossis must have put it in long after the house was built, for Nicole to swim laps. The container, which was nothing more than a steel box welded to a trailer, was on the opposite side of the pool. He opened the door and a storage carton fell out. There was plenty of room inside the container, but it looked like it had been organized by Poco. The only way to fix it was to take everything out and start all over again.

Chase looked up at the sky. Clouds were moving in from the gulf. He jogged down to the Shop, imitating Tomás's perpetual state of emergency, which is exactly what Chase would be in if it started to rain after he pulled everything out. He grabbed a couple of tarps, a hammer, and a handful of metal stakes.

Since they'd been on the road, his father had taken the Boy Scouts' motto, "Be Prepared," to a new level. Every job, no matter how small, needed to be thought through before it was started, from beginning to end, with particular attention paid to what might go wrong *in between*.

Chase staked out a ground tarp so it wouldn't blow away, then staged a second tarp to pull over the boxes in case it started to rain. What he neglected to anticipate in between was his curiosity about the Rossi family and their circus. In almost every box, he found something he had to look at or read.

There were stacks of photo albums filled with pictures of the big top, circus acts, animals, and people. Nicole's mom was a little person, like Momma Rossi and Marco. Others in the family were regular size, like Nicole. But in every photo, they were smiling and laughing as if there wasn't an inch of difference between them.

Marco walked up as Chase was staring at a painting of a man holding a whip, dressed in a red coat, white pants, knee-high black boots, and a black top hat.

"That's my great-grandfather, Ricardo Rossi. He was a famous ringmaster in Europe before he came over here to start his own circus. The picture doesn't show his stature in perspective very well. He was four inches shorter than I am. He died when I was five years old. He was ninety-six. The day before he died he was in the ring, training a stallion."

"Wow."

"Yep, he was quite a guy." Marco looked at the tarp and boxes. "Did Momma Rossi give you this chore?"

"No," Chase answered. "I offered to help. I'm supposed to be organizing and repacking everything, but I guess what I'm doing mostly is snooping."

Marco laughed. "Hard not to. A lot of interesting history here." He reached into one of the boxes and pulled out a photograph of a man sitting on top of an elephant. "This is my dad. He was killed by an elephant when I was thirteen. He was quite a guy too."

"I'm sorry."

"Thanks. It was a long time ago, but I still miss him. Some things you just don't get over, I guess."

Chase understood this all too well. He'd wondered if he was ever going to get over the deaths of his mom and Monica. "But you still like elephants?"

"They're my favorite animal. They were my dad's favorite too." Marco looked at the container. "Think this will do the trick?"

"It's not really waterproof, Mr. Rossi," Chase answered.

"First, it's Marco, not Mr. Rossi. Second, can you waterproof it? Your dad said you were pretty handy."

"I can caulk it, and tarp it, which should keep the water out, but I think the boxes would be a lot safer back in the house."

"Not according to my mother," Marco said. "She's convinced the house is coming down."

"What do you think?"

"I don't agree with her on this, but she's my mother, and she's usually right."

Chase nodded. She was certainly right about the accident and his being a Boy Scout.

"Did Arturo tell you anything about us?"

"Like what?"

"Our past. Where we're from."

"All he said was that you helped people during storms and that you needed a place to hook up your rigs. Is there something else I should know?"

Chase shook his head. "I guess not."

"I better get back down to Pet and see what she's up to. Thanks for taking care of the container. I'll see you at dinner."

It took Chase nearly two hours to reload the container. When he finally got the last box inside, he caulked all the seams, threw the tarps over the top, and began securing them with bungee cords.

Nicole came out the back door of the house as he was stretching the last cord. "Why so many bungees?" she asked.

"So it doesn't float to the sun."

"Funny. It looks like a giant Christmas present wrapped in blue paper."

"It won't leak."

"I'll say."

"How's the sweet potato pie?"

"It's perfect."

Chase smiled. "I suppose anyone who scratches lions under the chin is entitled to a certain amount of confidence. I better go down to the Shack and get cleaned up before dinner."

"Hurry," Nicole said. "Sweet potato pie is terrible when it's cold."

As Chase was drying his hair in the Shack's kitchen, he realized that they didn't have a single photograph hanging up, from either their former or current life.

How can that be? Where are the photos of Mom and Monica? The notebooks with Monica's stories and drawings?

They weren't in the fifth-wheel or the semitrailer. Chase knew exactly what they had, and where all of it was stored.

What's Dad done with our past?

07:42 PM

Chase sat with the Rossis in their kitchen in front of enough food to feed a bunkhouse of roughnecks for a week. Pork chops, fried chicken, garlic mashed potatoes, a trough of Caesar salad, steamed beans, fresh baked rolls, and of course sweet potato pie — all delicious, especially the pie. It might have been the best meal he'd ever eaten. It was certainly the most entertaining, with the Rossis telling him story after story of their life in the circus, pausing once in a while to glance over at Emily on the television. . . .

"Emily has all the makings of a Category Five hurricane. The question is, Where is she going to make landfall and when? For the very latest information let's go to our meteorologist, Cindy Stewart. Cindy?"

"Well, Richard, it's a little premature to say Emily's going to be a Category Five hurricane, but she is gathering strength. Right now Emily is stalled about one hundred fifty miles southwest of here with sustained winds in

excess of one hundred thirty-one miles per hour, making her a Category Four at the moment, which is still a potentially devastating storm. Anything in her path is going to be in for a severe pounding."

"Any idea what her path is going to be?"

"No. We'll have a better idea when Emily starts to move, but even then, she could switch directions. At this point it's up to fate...."

That word again, Chase thought.

Marco took another scoop of sweet potato pie. His appetite was anything but small.

"Looks like you'll have school tomorrow," he said.

"Are you kidding?" Nicole said. "You can't do everything here by yourself."

"Chase will be here."

"Actually, I won't be here," Chase said. "If Nicole has school, I have school."

"And there's that little problem called a Category Five hurricane coming our way," Nicole added. "Besides, what about Pet? If you think I'm going to miss an elephant birth, you're crazy."

Marco held up a thumb. "I'm not completely crazy." Index finger. "Emily's not a Category Five . . . yet." Middle finger. "We don't know Emily's coming this way." Ring finger. "Pet might not calve for weeks." Little finger. Marco looked at Momma Rossi as if he couldn't think of a fifth reason. "What do you think?"

"I think if there is school, you both need to go. School is important." She glanced at the TV, then added with an eerie certainty, "After the hurricane, there won't be school for a long time."

Nicole walked Chase back to the Shack & Shop. He gave her a tour, which didn't take long. As she was leaving, she paused and asked, "Why do you always carry your backpack with you? This seems like a safe enough place to leave it, but when we were having dinner, you had it right at your feet."

"Emergencies. If I get separated or stuck someplace, it has everything I need to keep me going for a few days. My dad calls it a go bag. We all carry one."

"It must be strange to travel around from one disaster to another."

"It's probably not that different from being in a circus."

"You might be right," Nicole agreed.

"What time does the bus come?"

"Seven ten."

"Early."

"We're almost the farthest from town."

"I can drive us down to the road on the quad," Chase offered.

"Great." Nicole gave him smile. "I'll see you tomorrow morning."

Chase watched Nicole walk away and wondered what his father would say if he told him he wanted to become a lion tamer.

05:46 AM

Chase pulled on a pair of cargo pants, T-shirt, and tennis shoes, then listened to the weather on the radio as he ate breakfast. Emily was stalled in the Gulf of Mexico, gathering strength, making up her mind which way to go.

His cell phone rang.

"What time is it?" his father asked.

"Six o'clock . . . exactly."

"That's what I thought."

"How do I know you're not looking at the time on your cell phone?"

"Because your old man wouldn't lie to you. How are things there?"

"I'm getting ready for school."

"Good."

"Uh . . . I'm kind of curious about something."

"What's that?"

"I was wondering where all our old photos are . . . you know, of the family."

"I gave them to your uncle Bob for safekeeping. We don't have a lot of room in the Shack, and storing them in the places we go is a good way to lose them. What made you think about that?"

"I don't know. Maybe hearing the name Emily over and over again."

His father was silent for several seconds, then said, "I can see that. But the name's just a coincidence. They alternate female and male names every hurricane season, starting with the letter *A*. This year it's been Arlene, Bret, Cindy, Don, and now Emily. I better get going. Tomás is over at the restaurant. Everything okay?"

"Yeah."

"Stay alert, Chase."

"I will."

"Talk to you later."

His father ended the call.

07:45AM

The school bus slowed down several times along the route but didn't stop because there was no one waiting to be picked up. When they finally arrived at Palm Breeze Middle School the bus was only half full.

The first time Chase had enrolled himself in a new school he'd been nervous. By the third school it had gotten a lot easier. This time, with Nicole leading him into the office, it was no big deal at all.

She introduced him to the receptionist, Mrs. O'Leary.

"Chase is staying with us," she said. "His dad is helping people get ready for the hurricane."

This was not exactly what Chase's father was doing, but he didn't correct her.

Mrs. O'Leary peered at Chase above her reading glasses. "Your dad knows where the hurricane is going to hit?"

"Not really. He's just guessing like everyone else."

"What's his guess for Emily?"

"Forty or fifty miles south of here in Saint Petersburg — Saint Pete."

"I hope he's right. Though if the absentee rate is any

indication, a lot of parents are guessing differently. Do you have your academic transcripts from your previous school?"

Chase pulled a folder out of his go bag. Attached to the folder was a note from his father with his cell number in case they needed to get in touch with him. No school had ever called him.

"Take a seat, Chase. Our principal, Dr. Krupp, will talk to you after she gets off the phone."

"I'll see you later," Nicole said with a smile, then joined friends out in the hallway.

After about ten minutes, Dr. Krupp stepped out of her office and invited Chase in.

He sat down on the opposite side of her huge desk. As she skimmed his paperwork he looked around her office.

"Did Nicole's brother go to school here?" Chase asked.

Dr. Krupp looked up from the folder. "Tony? Yes, he was an outstanding student and a wonderful athlete. Nicole is following in his footsteps, but the pool is her football field. Is Tony in town?"

"No. I was just looking at your diplomas and noticed that you went to the University of Georgia, where he plays."

Dr. Krupp smiled for the first time. "Yes, Tony's a Bulldog. I like to think that I had something to do with that, but he made up his own mind. The Rossis are an independent bunch, but you probably already know that."

Normally, Chase would have let her hold on to her assumption that he knew the Rossis well, but he was getting tired of *tries*. That's what his mother had called a statement or even a silence that was not quite the truth and not exactly a lie. When Chase, or anyone in the family, pulled one on her, she'd say, "Nice *trie*, now try again."

"I just met the Rossis yesterday," Chase said.

"Really?" Dr. Krupp said. "Mrs. O'Leary led me to believe that you were old family friends."

"We are friends," Chase said. "But we're new friends."

"Are you in the animal or circus business?"

Chase shook his head. "We're in the storm business. My father's a contractor."

"For the government?"

"No, for himself."

"M.D. Emergency Services." Dr. Krupp glanced at the file, then back at Chase. "Is he a doctor and a contractor?"

"No," Chase said. "Just a contractor."

"We usually have one or both parents bring their kids in when they enroll them," Dr. Krupp said.

"My father's working in Saint Pete," Chase said. "My mom died a couple of years ago. It's just me and him now."

"I'm sorry about your mom, Chase."

"Thanks."

Dr. Krupp's phone rang and she picked it up. While she talked, Chase looked at the photos of Dr. Krupp's family. Three kids and a husband who looked like a movie star, which surprised him. Dr. Krupp was okay-looking, but far from glamorous. And for some reason, her husband looked familiar, but Chase couldn't remember where he had seen the man before.

Dr. Krupp hung up the phone. "Now, where were we?"

"You can call my dad if you want," Chase said. "He always answers his cell."

His dad carried a beat-up cell phone on a lanyard around his neck so he could get to it without having to reach into his pocket. It looked geeky to Chase, and his mom had hated "the phone necklace," as she'd called it, but it was practical. His dad usually answered the phone on the first or second ring.

"That won't be necessary," Dr. Krupp said. "I'm sure he's busy or he'd be here with you."

Not necessarily, Chase thought.

Dr. Krupp handed him his class schedule and his locker combination. "This is a good school, Chase. You'll like it here."

08:20 AM

Dr. Krupp had put Chase in all of Nicole's classes, except PE, starting with Mrs. Sprague's homeroom.

For as much work as they were doing in homeroom, Chase thought they might as well have canceled school. A third of the desks were empty. The television mounted to the ceiling was tuned to the Weather Channel.

At 8:45 AM Emily started to move.

While everyone stared up at the screen to watch the white whirl of destruction headed their way, Chase looked out the window. This is what people did in the old days before satellite imagery and Doppler radar.

When they'd arrived at Palm Breeze Middle School an hour earlier, the sky had been clear, with no wind. Now it was flat gray. Dead palm fronds were tumbling across the soccer field out back. Chase began to get a strange feeling about Emily and wondered if this was what his dad experienced when he made his predictions, or what a lightning rod felt just before a strike. A tingling sensation. A spark of premonition . . .

"Last night Emily was upgraded to a Category Four hurricane with sustained winds of up to one hundred fifty-five miles per hour. There is a chance she'll become a Category Five, but what's even more disturbing is the speed at which she's traveling.

"Although hurricane winds can exceed one hundred miles an hour, the storm itself usually travels about fifteen miles an hour. This is one of the reasons hurricanes cause so much damage when they hit land. Instead of moving through quickly, they linger, giving the high winds time to cause severe damage.

"Emily is currently barreling toward the west coast of Florida at thirty-five miles per hour. We have accurate tracking records going back decades, and this speed is simply unheard of.

"On her current track and speed she will be making landfall near the Tampa-Saint Pete area around eleven this evening. . . ."

About forty miles south of Palm Breeze Middle School, just like Dad predicted. Chase continued to stare out the window. He still had that tingling feeling, and it contradicted what he was hearing from the television and what he was seeing out the window. Although the wind wasn't even close to hurricane strength, he had a weird feeling that Momma Rossi was closer to the mark than his dad or any of the experts.

Mrs. Sprague switched the TV to a local station, and a familiar face appeared on the screen. It was the anchor they had watched during dinner the night before. Chase realized why the photos of Dr. Krupp's husband looked familiar.

He turned to Nicole and whispered, "Is that —"

"Yeah, that's Dr. Krupp's husband. All the teachers really like him. He comes to talk to us every year." She leaned closer. "I think he's a little strange. He wears more makeup than Dr. Krupp even when he's talking to us."

Chase doubted that the morning news was Richard Krupp's regular beat. He was the prime-time anchor.

Chase and his father always got a big kick out of watching television reporters during disasters. They'd say they hoped the storm would pass them, but the truth was that they wanted to be right in the middle of it with their Gore-Tex gear, leaning into the wind, dodging debris, telling everyone how dangerous it was. If the reporters were unlucky and the storm hit elsewhere, they'd insert themselves into the story by jumping into their satellite vans and driving there, as if the town where the disaster struck actually needed more reporters.

Richard Krupp wasn't in his Gore-Tex yet, but Chase was certain he would be before long. His hair was a little disheveled, and it looked as if he hadn't shaved since the night before. He was wearing jeans and hiking boots, the sleeves to his sky blue dress shirt rolled up to just below the elbow. Emily loomed behind him in high definition like a circular saw looking for something to cut in two.

Richard Krupp was unafraid. He stared into the camera, trying to look concerned, but his shining blue eyes gave him away. He was excited.

> "... looks like we're in for a rough night, but the important thing to remember is not to panic. At this point, state police and local law enforcement are not calling for mandatory evacuation, but they are suggesting that if you have somewhere to stay outside of Emily's projected track, you should proceed there after securing your property.
>
> "The news team and I will of course be here for the duration. . . ."

Of course. Chase looked at his new classmates. They were all glued to the screen, hanging on Richard Krupp's every word.

> "Let's go to our meteorologist, Cindy Stewart, in downtown Saint Pete and see what the mood is there. Cindy?"
>
> "As you can see, Richard, a few clouds have moved in and the wind has picked

up slightly, but honestly, if we weren't look-
ing at the satellite images behind you, we
wouldn't know that a hurricane was headed
this way. . . ."

Richard Krupp looked irritated.

"But there is a hurricane coming, Cindy. A
big one."

"There's no doubt about that, Richard, but
due to Emily's erratic behavior, we're still
unclear about where she'll make landfall.
Because of the speed she's traveling, even
a slight deviation from the path she's on
could put her hundreds of miles away from
Saint Pete."

"But not away from Florida."

"That's right, Richard. She's going to hit
Florida."

Richard gave her a triumphant look. Cindy rolled her eyes
slightly, but continued to smile. Chase was beginning to really
like her. He would love to see these two in the news station
lunchroom. He suspected their relationship was a lot worse
off camera.

"So, is there anyone downtown making
preparations for the storm, Cindy?"

"Yes, there's a lot of activity down here. As you attempted to say earlier, it doesn't hurt to be cautious."

The camera zoomed out and Chase's jaw dropped open at what he saw on the television screen.

M.D. EMERGENCY SERVICES

The camera zoomed back a little more, revealing John Masters leaning against his 4x4.

Nicole turned to Chase and said loudly, "Isn't that your father's truck?"

"Yeah," Chase said. "And that's him leaning against it."

The whole class stared at him.

"Your dad's hot," a girl said.

"What's that hanging around his neck?" someone else asked.

If Chase could have climbed out the window without anyone noticing, he would have.

"It's a cell phone," Chase answered.

"That's kind of geeky."

"He's still hot."

Chase had never thought of his dad as hot, but he had to admit that, except for the cell phone around his neck, his dad did look pretty good. He was wearing faded jeans, scuffed work boots, and a sleeveless T-shirt that showed off his tan and well-defined biceps and forearms. Strapped around his narrow waist was his favorite tool belt.

Mrs. Sprague turned up the volume. "Settle down, everyone. Let's hear what Chase's father has to say."

Chase wasn't sure what to expect, but his father looked perfectly at ease in front of the camera, as if he'd been on TV every day of his life. He hadn't even been on the local news after the lightning strike. Dozens of shows had called asking him to appear, but he had turned them all down. Chase had thought at the time that his father was camera shy. He was obviously wrong.

> *"I'm standing next to John Masters, owner of M.D. Emergency Services. What are you doing down here, John?"*
>
> *"Helping out . . . making sure the damage will be minimal if Emily hits here."*
>
> *"And what makes you think Emily is going to hit Saint Pete?"*
>
> *"She may not, but she is headed this direction and this is where I happen to be."*
>
> *"And why do you happen to be in Saint Pete?"*
>
> *"I've never been here before. Always wanted to come. Bad timing, I guess."*

Bad trie, *Dad*, Chase thought.

> *"Show us what you've been doing."*

Chase's father walked Cindy through taping and boarding up windows, securing or removing anything that might get caught by the wind, moving valuables to the upper floors. . . .

> *"In case of storm surge?"*
>
> *"That's right, Cindy. Just like we saw in Hurricane Katrina. If your house or building is standing after the wind, flooding is the next problem. Water damage can be worse than wind damage . . . much worse . . . and with all the oil floating around the gulf from the BP spill, there could be a real mess here on shore."*

The interview was interrupted by the voice of Mrs. O'Leary over the intercom. She called about twenty students down to the office, saying their parents were waiting to pick them up. Four kids from Mrs. Sprague's class. By the time they gathered their things and left, Richard Krupp was back on the screen, trying to look worried but brave.

12:15 PM

Chase called his father during lunch. He answered on the first ring.

"Twelve fifteen. How's it going?"

"You're right about the time, and I'm fine," Chase said. "I saw you on TV."

"At school?"

"Yeah. In a classroom."

"That must have been a surprise."

"It was." Chase wondered if his father would have even told him if Chase hadn't mentioned it first. "Cindy Stewart seems cool."

"She is."

"It doesn't sound like she thinks Emily is going to hit down there."

"She might be right. And if she is, we may have to move the Shack and Shop closer to Emily's track. Tomás and I will stay here tonight, but if Emily misses us we'll be heading up your way first thing in the morning to get you and pick up the rigs."

Great, Chase thought. *A new record. One day in one school.*

"That might not be as easy as you think," Chase said.

"What do you mean?"

"The clouds have moved in and the wind's been picking up all morning." Chase hesitated. "I think Emily is going to hit up here." This was followed by a long pause on his father's end of the line. It went on so long that Chase thought the call had been dropped. "Are you there?"

"Yep, I'm here. What other evidence do you have?"

"Nothing scientific, if that's what you mean." Chase didn't want to get into Momma Rossi's soothsaying. "It's just a feeling I have."

"Have they canceled school?"

"No, but a lot of parents have picked their kids up. The principal is married to that Richard guy on TV."

His father laughed. "Cindy's not too fond of him. You should have heard what she had to say off camera about Saint Pete's Number One News Anchor."

"What about Emily?" Chase asked.

"I don't know. They're still predicting that it's going to hit down here, but at this point, your guess is as good as anyone else's. You want us to head up tonight?"

"I guess not," Chase said. "You're already set up down there. If you come up here and I'm wrong, you might not be able to get back in."

Roads were often closed during a disaster, which was why his father liked to be at ground zero beforehand.

"You know the drill. If you think someone's making a bonehead decision, don't go along with them. Remember that

57

you've had more experience with storms than they have. Stick with what I've taught you. Do what you think is right. If the storm hits up there, save yourself. You're no good to anybody if you're dead . . . including yourself."

Chase could not remember how many times his father had said these exact words to him.

"I will."

His father continued in a lighter tone. "I didn't get to ask you this morning, but what's the farm like?"

"It's a circus."

"Wild, huh?"

"Literally." It was obvious his father had no idea what Chase meant.

"That's great. Well, I better get back to work. Keep an eye on that weather. Call me this evening." He ended the call.

Nicole walked up. "Who were you talking to?"

"My father."

"What did he say about his television appearance?"

"Not much."

"He's probably used to it by now."

"As far as I know, that's the first time he's been on TV."

"Really? I would think he'd be on all the time, considering what he does for a living."

It's now or never, Chase thought. No more *tries.* Especially with Nicole. "How long before we have to be back to class?"

"About twenty minutes. Why?"

Chase started with his mother's and sister's deaths, then moved on to the lightning strike and M.D. Emergency Services, and ended with their arrival at the Rossi Brothers' winter quarters. He skipped a few things, like his father storing away all the evidence of their former life.

Nicole listened without saying a word until he finished.

"I've never met anyone struck by lightning."

"That's not surprising. Most people don't survive lightning strikes. Believe me, it's no fun to see someone struck by lightning."

"Especially your own father," Nicole said. "Does he have any other . . . uh . . . ill effects from the strike?"

"You mean besides selling everything we own, becoming a nomad, and charging desperate people a ton of cash to help them?"

Nicole grinned. "Yes, besides that."

"When he got out of the hospital, he got his ear pierced."

Nicole laughed. "That sounds more like a midlife crisis."

"Except for the fact that he had a jeweler melt down his gold wedding band and turn it into a lightning bolt earring."

"That's a little strange," Nicole admitted.

03:33 PM

Throughout the afternoon, parents arrived to pick up their kids. Several came with their SUVs packed, ready to head out of the storm area. The teachers seemed eager to leave too, especially the ones with children.

By the time the final bell rang, there were only a hundred students left in the building. More than half of them had parents waiting for them at the curb, leaving only forty-two bus riders to put on nine buses.

Dr. Krupp thought it was ridiculous to send out that many buses with so few students — an opinion all the bus drivers agreed with.

"The traffic's terrible."

"It's the worst jam I've ever seen."

"The highways are like parking lots."

Dr. Krupp drafted the two most experienced drivers to take the remaining forty-two students home in two buses.

While they were figuring out who to put on which bus, Chase stared up at the sky. He didn't like what he saw. The clouds were an angry swollen gray and looked like they were about to burst.

"What time does it usually get dark around here?" he asked Nicole.

"Seven thirty or eight," she answered. "Why?"

He looked at his watch. "It's three forty and look how dark it is."

"You're right. It looks like it's going to rain."

"It's going to do a lot worse than that." He looked back up at the sky and was tempted to call his father again.

Instead he said loudly, "What's the latest on Emily?"

He hadn't seen a weather report for a couple of hours, but he estimated that the wind was blowing at least fifteen miles an hour where they were standing, and gusting to twenty-five or thirty. The thick, bruised clouds above were moving fast.

No one answered him. He asked again. Louder.

This time everyone turned his way.

Dr. Krupp looked annoyed. "I talked to my husband fifteen minutes ago. He said that Emily is going to hit south of here around midnight."

"How far south?"

"No one knows."

"What category?"

"Right now it's a Category Five. But they're predicting Emily will be downgraded back to a Category Four by the time she makes landfall."

"I heard it's gonna be a Category Three," one of the bus drivers added.

"That's still winds in excess of one hundred miles an hour," Chase said. "I don't think the buses are a good idea."

Dr. Krupp put her hands on her hips. "Really? And how do you suggest we get you and the other students home?"

"I don't think we should go home. We should stay right here. The school has a low profile. The buildings are constructed out of reinforced concrete. The safest thing for us to do is to ride out the storm in the cafetorium. It's right in the middle of the campus, no windows, protected on all four sides by other buildings."

"How long have you been in Florida, Chase?" Dr. Krupp asked.

Here we go, Chase thought. He took a deep breath. "Two days."

"And how many hurricanes have you been in?"

"None, but I know enough to stay exactly where I am when I have everything I need to survive."

"You're getting on the bus, Chase. We are not spending the night at the school. We don't have authorization from the district, or your parents. Getting permission would take several hours." She looked at her watch. "You'll all be home in less than two hours."

Nicole stepped forward. Chase didn't want her to get involved. This was his argument.

"Let me talk to him, Dr. Krupp."

"Make it quick. You're leaving in two minutes."

Dr. Krupp walked back to the drivers. The kids stared at Chase like he had lost his mind. One of them made clucking noises like a chicken. Chase took a step toward the boy, but

Nicole grabbed his arm and pulled him down a breezeway where no one could hear them.

"What do you think you're doing, Chase?"

"You're mad at *me*?" He couldn't believe it. He'd expected Nicole to be on his side, but she looked more upset than Dr. Krupp.

"Dr. Krupp is trying to get everyone home safely and you're —"

"Dr. Krupp is trying to get us out of her hair so *she* can go home. She doesn't want to spend the night with forty-two kids in the cafetorium."

"That's right! She wants to spend the night with her own family just like I do. Just like everyone here does. Just because you don't have —" Nicole stopped herself.

"You think this is about me?" Chase asked.

"Who else would it be about?"

"It's about all of us. We are leaving a perfect place to ride out a hurricane. The two buses are going to take us to homes that are not nearly as safe as Palm Breeze Middle School. That is, if we even make it home. Everyone is talking about where the hurricane is going to make landfall." Chase pointed at the ground. "I've got news for you. It's going to be here. Right where we're standing. And it will be here a long time before midnight. Dr. Krupp cannot make anyone get on a bus. If we stick together we can stay at the school, where we'll be safe."

"You can spend the night here if you want," Nicole said.

"But I'm getting on the bus and going home. You are being paranoid!"

Chase watched her stamp back to the curb and the waiting buses. He thought about the farmer in Oklahoma who left his combine in the middle of the hailstorm. He'd been going home too. He'd made it about a hundred yards before being stoned to death. He'd gotten hit in the head twice. The first stone knocked him out. The second killed him, according to the newspaper.

Dr. Krupp started dividing the forty-two students into two groups. Chase thought about holding his ground and refusing to go, but it wouldn't accomplish anything. She would still put the other kids on the buses and send them on their way, including Nicole. Dr. Krupp would stay behind with him and either call his father and tell him to pick Chase up, or call the police and have them deal with him.

Going against everything he knew, everything his father had taught him, he joined the others at the curb, ignoring the smirks and clucking sounds. He wasn't about to let Nicole ride on the bus without him.

"Mrs. O'Leary is calling your parents to tell them you might be a little late because of the alternate route, the traffic, and the weather so they don't worry."

Chase was the last to board his bus. As he stepped through the door, Dr. Krupp put her hand on his shoulder.

"There's nothing to worry or be nervous about, Chase. Don't be afraid. You'll be at the Rossis' farm in no time at all."

"There is everything to be worried about, Dr. Krupp." He pointed at the sky. "Emily is here. You'd better drive straight home and stay away from windows."

Chase realized that Dr. Krupp was trying to be kind, but being kind didn't make someone right. He was not afraid to ride on a bus. But there wasn't time to explain to her what his father called The Gut Barometer, or TGB. "Everyone has one," his father had told him. "It works just like a real barometer: When the pressure drops, the weather is going to change. The TGB is in your solar plexus. You feel the pressure drop in your gut." Most of the time people ignored their gut gauge, and most of the time it was okay to ignore it, until the one time it wasn't okay.

Chase knew this was one of those times.

He got on the bus, and the driver pulled the door closed behind him. The kids had all paired off and were grinning at him as he made his way past them. Nicole had taken an aisle seat next to some guy and didn't even glance at him as he walked by.

"Cluck . . . cluck . . . cluck . . . ," someone said from the front of the bus.

A few kids laughed.

Chase took the bench seat at the back of the bus. Right next to the emergency exit.

05:15 PM

"Does anyone have a cell signal?"

Three hours before nightfall, it was almost completely dark outside.

Chase sat in the back and watched the lights as sixteen cell phones flicked on. They had been on the bus an hour and a half and had dropped off four people. He knew there wasn't a cell signal because he'd been checking his phone since they'd left the school. He wanted to talk to his father, and thought about breaking out the satellite phone, but it was only to be used in case of emergency. And in order for it to work, his father would have to have his satellite phone on, which was unlikely at this point in the storm.

"No signal."

"No bars."

"Dead as a doornail."

Gusts of wind crashed into the bus like ocean waves as they inched along in bumper-to-bumper traffic. The rain poured down so hard it was pointless to look out the window. All they could see were headlights and glimpses of angry motorists.

The bus stopped again. The kid next to Nicole got up, along with four others, and they made their way to the front.

"Okay!" the driver shouted. "Do you see your parents' cars out there?"

The kids peered through the steamed windows. They said they did.

"Are you sure? 'Cause I'm not letting you off this bus unless you do. I don't care how close your house is to this stop. You can't walk in this stuff. If your folks aren't there, I'll drive you to your doorstep."

They all swore their parents were waiting.

"Okay. On the count of three I'll pull the door open and you all bail out quickly so I don't get too drenched. One . . . two . . . three . . ." The doors shuddered open and the kids jumped out into the wind and rain like paratroopers.

The driver got soaked anyway to everyone's amusement, except Chase's.

Chase noticed Nicole move over into the window seat vacated by the boy. Why? She wouldn't be able to see out, and it was more dangerous to sit near the window than the aisle. He knew he should make his way up to her and say something, but the only things he had to say would sound wimpy, so he stayed where he was, thinking about how dangerous school buses were. At his last school he'd done a report on them and gotten an A, but the teacher had said it would be best not to put it up on the bulletin board with the other reports because it might scare people.

School buses are not designed to operate in winds exceeding fifty miles an hour. Even on a calm day, school buses aren't safe. In every state, it's against the law to drive in a car without a seat belt. By law, children under a certain weight have to ride in the back, strapped into an appropriate car seat or booster. Parents wait with their kids at the bus stop so nothing bad happens to them, then they watch them climb into the yellow death trap and blow them kisses good-bye.

Florida is one of the few states that require seat belts in school buses, but only in newer school buses. The Palm Breeze bus was not new. The driver was the only one belted in.

Wimp, Chase thought. But he couldn't help himself. Over the past year he'd seen too many disasters and what happened when people didn't recognize them for what they were. The kids on the bus thought this was an adventure. But Chase knew it was just the beginning of what, for some of them, would be the worst night of their lives.

07:10 PM

The wind got stronger and the rain fell harder. When there were just five of them left on the bus, Nicole finally joined Chase on the back bench.

"This is pretty scary. You might have been right about staying at school."

"We're almost at the farm, aren't we?"

Nicole started talking very quickly. "I can't tell. The driver's been following a crazy route to get around traffic. The girl sitting right behind the driver lives the closest to us. I think her name's Rashawn. She's a new girl. Someone told me her father's the caretaker of the wildlife refuge next to our farm. The caretaker's house is five miles farther out. She's usually already on the bus when I get on in the morning. I guess her parents took her to school today. She's probably wishing they had picked her up too. . . . I'm sorry I called you paranoid."

Chase smiled. Not at Nicole's nervousness but at something his father had said to his uncle Bob when Uncle Bob accused him of being paranoid.

"I wasn't insulted," Chase said. "Paranoia is just another word for heightened awareness."

"Funny," Nicole said, relaxing . . . a little. "Why are you sitting way back here?"

Chase pointed at the emergency door. "Safer."

The bus stopped. Two more people jumped off, leaving Chase, Nicole, and the girl sitting up front.

"Tell me about the refuge," Chase said, as the bus lurched forward. He didn't really care about the refuge, but he felt that if he could keep her talking, it might calm her down.

"It borders one end of our farm. We actually used to own a good piece of the refuge land, but my grandfather donated it to the state."

"How big is it?"

"It's huge, and getting bigger. The state bought a large parcel of land down the road from us with a levee on it. Eventually they'll buy our place, which will connect the levee property to the refuge."

"Your dad's going to sell the farm?"

"Not any time soon, but yeah, he'll sell it. If the circus goes under, we won't need the land."

"What's on the refuge?"

"I haven't really spent any time there. If I'm not swimming, I'm taking care of the animals. There isn't much time for exploring. I suppose the refuge has birds, gators, deer, snakes . . . Florida things."

Chase scooted over to the window. All he could see was pitch-black through sheets of rain, no car lights, no streetlights, no house lights. He scooted back to Nicole.

"Maybe we should invite Rashawn to come back here with us. She's probably just as scared as we are."

"You're scared?"

"Yeah, aren't you?"

"I'll get her."

Chase pulled the handheld GPS out of his go bag and fired it up.

Nicole returned with Rashawn. She was big, almost as tall as he was. She was sopping wet from sitting close to the door, and she was shivering. He hoped she was shivering because she was cold, not frightened. None of them was dressed for a hurricane. Rashawn sat down on the bench across the aisle from them. Chase took a Mylar first aid blanket out of his bag and handed it to her.

"Why're you sitting all the way back here?" Rashawn asked through chattering teeth.

"Chase thinks it's safe —"

"Warmer," Chase interrupted. No use scaring Rashawn any more than she was. "And drier."

"You're the boy who was afraid to get on the bus."

"Yeah."

Rashawn shook the blanket out and put it around her broad shoulders. "What kind of kid carries a blanket in his backpack?"

"A Boy Scout," Nicole answered.

"Former Boy Scout," Chase clarified.

"That bus driver's lost," Rashawn said.

"What makes you think that?" Chase asked.

"Been sitting behind him since we left school. He talks to himself. He also curses . . . a lot. Everything was fine until he dumped off those last two kids. He took what he thought was a shortcut."

"Do you know where we are?"

Rashawn shook her head, splashing water from her wet hair on both of them. "I've only been here a month. I couldn't find my way home from school on a bet. Guess I should have been paying better attention."

Chase slid over to the window to get a better angle on the satellites for his GPS. Once the satellite located them he could he could punch in where they needed to go and tell the driver.

"Maybe we can help him."

07:20 PM

Their location popped up on the little screen, but it meant nothing to Chase. As he turned to ask Nicole for her address, a gust of wind lifted the bus completely off its tires. Just as suddenly, the bus slammed back on the road and started to tip.

"On the floor!" Chase shouted above Rashawn's and Nicole's screams. He reached out and grabbed an arm — he couldn't tell who it belonged to — and pulled one of the girls to the floor. "Brace yourselves!" He wrapped his legs and arms around the steel seat rods, hoping Nicole and Rashawn had done the same. If they were lucky, the bus would simply land on its side.

They weren't lucky.

The bus rolled three times, maybe four. . . . It was impossible to tell in the dark with the deafening sound of screeching metal, shattering windows, and terrified screams — including Chase's own.

The bus came to a stop, but only long enough for Chase to reach out and grab his GPS. He glanced at the screen and saw a single black line surrounded by blue.

The bus started to slide. Front end first.

"We're going into the water!" he shouted, hoping someone

was alive to hear him. "Stay on this end of the bus! We'll use the emergency exit!"

No one responded. They were either too frightened to speak, unconscious, dead, or had tumbled to the front of the bus.

The bus hit the water like a torpedo, pushing Chase's face into the seat frame. He felt a front tooth snap, followed by the coppery taste of blood. Frantically he felt around for his go bag. He'd need the first aid kit and everything else in the bag if they survived the crash.

He grabbed a handful of hair.

"Ouch!"

Chase spit out a mouthful of blood. "Nicole?"

"Yeah."

"Anything broken?"

"I don't think so. You?"

"Front tooth. Where's Rashawn?"

"I'm next to Nicole," Rashawn said.

"My go bag," Chase said.

"I have it," Nicole said. "We're sinking."

"Give me the bag."

Chase pulled a headlamp out of the side pocket, turned it on, and slipped it over his forehead. Nicole looked pale in the bright light.

"You and Rashawn go through the emergency door and get to shore. It can't be too far."

He pulled a second headlamp out and handed it to her.

"What are you going to do?" Nicole asked, putting the headlamp on.

"I'm going to check on the driver."

They looked down the length the bus. Water was gushing through the cracked windshield.

"I'm a better swimmer," Nicole said.

"I'm sure you are," Chase said. "But I'm stronger."

"I'll go with you."

"No, get Rashawn to shore. I'll be right behind you. Go!"

The water was rising fast. The bus would be completely submerged within minutes. He made his way down the steep, slippery aisle, wondering how he was going to get the driver back up the aisle if the guy was unconscious.

The driver *was* unconscious, slumped over the steering wheel. Chase pulled him up. There was a deep, ugly gash on the man's forehead oozing blood.

Chase shouted at him, then tried to shake him awake.

No response.

After the lightning strike, he and his father had taken first aid classes three nights a week for months. By the time they'd finished they could have become paramedics.

He felt the man's neck for a pulse. He didn't feel one, but that didn't mean the driver was dead. Chase's hands were numb with cold. He felt his jagged tooth with his tongue and glanced up the aisle to the rear of the bus. Nicole had the emergency door open and was helping Rashawn through.

The water was up to the driver's chest now and rising fast. Chase shouted and gave him another shake. The driver let out a weak moan just as the front end of the bus plunged completely underwater.

Chase was washed backward in a rush of water. He managed to get a gulp of air just before he was slammed into one of the seats as the bus slipped sideways, then rolled. As the bus slid farther he pulled his way up to the driver again and grabbed the man's arm. He tried to yank the driver free of the seat, but he wouldn't budge.

Seat belt!

Chase wasted several precious seconds trying to find the release. If he didn't get the driver to the surface on his first try, the driver would drown. If he didn't get to the surface himself in about thirty seconds, *he* would drown. Chase shrugged the pack off his back and unzipped one of the pockets. The bus settled to the bottom with a dull *thump*.

Chase tried to keep the panic down. He couldn't afford to make a mistake. He pulled his knife out of the pocket and sliced the seat belt in two places. The driver rose from the seat like a balloon and came to a stop against the door, blocking the exit.

Chase knew he wouldn't make it to the emergency exit in the back of the bus with the driver in tow. That left the windshield. It was cracked in several places. He braced his back against a pole and was about to try to kick the windshield out, when something dark and very big swam past outside. Chase couldn't tell what it was, but it frightened him so badly that he nearly sucked in a lungful of water.

Get ahold of yourself! Oxygen deprivation is making you see things.

The windshield popped loose on the third kick. On the fourth it came out of the frame and dropped into the dark water. With his lungs screaming for air, Chase grabbed the driver by his shirt collar and pulled him through the opening.

Nicole was waiting for him.

As soon as she'd seen the bus sink, she'd dived back into the water, leaving Rashawn to make it to shore on her own. She'd gotten to the bus just as Chase was pulling the driver through the windshield. She grabbed Chase's free arm, wrapped it around her neck, and kicked toward the surface.

The second they broke the surface, Chase took a deep breath of air and started choking. Nicole helped him pull the driver's head above water.

"Can you swim on your own?" Nicole shouted.

Chase could barely hear her above the howling wind. He nodded.

Nicole wrapped her arm around the driver.

"Follow me. The shore's close."

They dragged the driver up on the bank where Rashawn was sitting huddled under the first aid blanket.

"We might need that blanket," Chase said.

Rashawn took the blanket off and gave it to Nicole. "Is he alive?"

"Not at the moment," Chase said, pushing the driver onto his stomach.

"What does that mean?"

Chase glimpsed his watch as he began pushing on the driver's back.

It was 7:32.

07:56PM

"Are you sure he's dead?" Rashawn asked.

Chase nodded.

No pulse. Dilated pupils. Instead of water, blood had come out of his mouth when Chase tried to resuscitate him, which meant he was probably dead before Chase cut the seat belt.

"I've never seen a dead person," Rashawn said.

Chase had seen more dead people than he cared to remember and wished he could have done more for the driver. But there were other priorities now. He didn't have time to think about what he might have been able to do, not now . . . except for one small detail, which he hated to bring up in front of Rashawn because she was already pretty freaked out.

"Are there alligators here?" he asked.

"That depends where here is," Nicole said.

"We're on the levee you were telling me about. Part of the refuge."

"Then there's gators," Rashawn said. "Thousands of them, according to my daddy, although I haven't been down on this part of the refuge."

Chase looked at Nicole. "Did you see one underwater?"

"No. Did you?"

"I think so. Just before I kicked the windshield out. I almost died right there. Thanks for coming back for me. I don't think I would have made it to the top on my own."

"Gators aren't nearly as aggressive as people think," Rashawn said.

"She's right," Nicole agreed. "You shouldn't mess with them, but they aren't usually a threat."

"Unless you stumble across a nest of gator eggs," Rashawn added. "Then you might have a big problem from the momma."

"I only saw it for a second, but something told me it was aggressive . . . very aggressive."

"Daddy's been dealing with gators forever," Rashawn said. "I suspect the gators are all riding out the storm on the bottom. The bus probably jarred one loose and it was popping up to get some air."

Chase was happy to hear Rashawn's little gator lecture. It meant she wasn't nearly as frightened as he'd thought she was. If they wanted to survive the storm, they could not panic. They had to keep their senses about them.

"It scared me," Chase said.

"Heightened awareness?" Nicole asked.

They would also have to keep their sense of humor.

"No," Chase said. "This time it was real paranoia. So, neither of you has been on this road?"

The road was about twenty feet above them, up a steep bank. The girls shook their heads.

"We have to find some shelter to ride out the storm," Chase said.

"It's not too bad right here," Rashawn said. "We're protected from the worst of the wind on this side of the levee."

"For now," Chase said. "But Emily's just getting started. The water's rising. It's gone up a foot since we've been sitting here."

He pulled the GPS out and turned it on. It was supposed to be waterproof, but the way their luck was going . . . The screen lit up and immediately picked up a satellite. Chase breathed a sigh of relief.

"What about your satellite phone?" Nicole asked.

His dad would certainly have his sat phone on now. "It's —" Chase felt his shoulder for the familiar strap. The go bag wasn't there. "I left it on the bus," he said. "The phone wasn't waterproof anyway and the bag was drenched. I guess I should dive back down and look for it. We could use some of the other stuff, like the first aid kit."

"I don't think that's a good idea," Rashawn said. "Gators aren't usually aggressive, but who knows what they're like in a hurricane."

Chase was beginning to really like Rashawn.

"You probably wouldn't find it anyway," Nicole said. "We have the headlamps and the GPS. The first aid kit would be nice, but . . ." She looked at his face. "Your lip is swollen and split. Are you okay?"

"I'm fine."

"Did you say something before we went down about your front tooth?"

"Yeah, but there's nothing in the first aid kit that's going to fix a tooth. I could use a painkiller, but that's the least of our worries."

He handed Nicole the GPS.

"This is the zoom button. Zoom out and find the nearest house. I'm going to check out the road."

Chase climbed up the bank, trying not to berate himself for failing to save the driver and forgetting the go bag. If he had the sat phone, and it worked, he'd be calling 9-1-1 right now and telling them where they were. Ninety percent of their problem would be over . . . maybe seventy-five percent. It would take a rescue team a while to get to them.

The wind was fiercer up on the road. He had to spread his legs as far as they would go and hunch over to keep from being blown back down the bank. He recalculated their chances of getting rescued even if they had the sat phone.

Ten percent, he thought.

He lumbered back to where the bus had gone into the water and discovered the wind had not blown it off the road. A large section of road was gone and water was rushing through the gap from the lake on the other side. It could have been the weight of the bus that caused the collapse, but he didn't think so. He walked forward a hundred yards and found another section of collapsed road.

Not good. *We need to get down this road while there's still a road to get down.*

He hurried to the spot he'd climbed up, and slid back down the bank.

Nicole and Rashawn were smiling.

"Did you find out where we are?"

"Right in the middle of the levee road," Nicole said. "A little less than five miles from the farm gate and ten miles from Rashawn's." She looked down at the driver, her smile fading. "He almost got us home."

"Are there any houses closer?" Chase asked.

Nicole shook her head. "Mine's the closest."

"Five miles isn't too bad," Chase said, not mentioning that walking five miles in a hurricane was probably like walking fifty miles.

"I bet my daddy's driving around, looking for me right now," Rashawn said.

"He's not driving this way," Chase said. "The road's collapsing. The only way to the farm is on foot. The good news is that there aren't any trees on the lake to fall on us, and there isn't much debris flying around. I had a couple of rain ponchos in the go bag, but —"

Nicole held up his go bag.

"Where —"

The girls' grins reappeared.

"I told her not to go," Rashawn said. "But she was in the water like a cormorant before I could stop her."

"What's a cormorant?"

"You don't know much about animals, do you?" Rashawn said. "It's a bird."

"It only took one dive," Nicole said. "It was right by the driver's seat."

"What about the gator?"

"Didn't see it. You must have scared it off."

Chase took the sat phone out and turned it on. Not surprisingly, it didn't work. Next he took out some energy bars and handed them out.

"I'm not hungry," Rashawn said. "We can eat when we get to Nicole's."

"Stick them in your pocket anyway," Chase said. "It will be a long time before we get to the farm." *If we get to the farm,* he thought. "They actually taste terrible, but they'll keep you going. We're going to burn a lot of energy in the next several hours."

Next he took out a bottle of water for each of them.

"I don't think water's going to be a problem," Nicole said, pointing to the sky.

"The water's falling on the outside of your body, not inside. We need to keep ourselves hydrated."

He took out a waterproof plastic bag with paper towels in it, wiped the sat phone down as best as he could, then put it in the plastic bag.

Finally he pulled out the two rain ponchos and handed one to each of the girls.

"What are you going to wear?" Rashawn asked. "Not that these are going to do us much good now. I'm soaked through."

"I'll use your blanket," Chase said. "It won't be as stylish as your ponchos, but it will work fine after I cut a hole for my head to fit through. I know you're wet, but the ponchos will help keep the wind out and your body heat in."

"You must be some kind of super Boy Scout," Rashawn said. "I've never seen a bag of tricks like that."

"It's a long story," Chase said.

"What about him?" Nicole asked, pointing to the driver.

Chase was sorry the man had died, very sorry, but he wanted to leave the driver exactly where he was. It would take a lot of energy they would need later to move him. "We can't take him with us," he said.

"We can't leave him here," Rashawn said. "Tomorrow morning after this storm passes, some ol' gator's going to come along and make a meal out of him."

"She's right," Nicole said.

"We'll drag him up to the road. High ground. That's the best we can do." Chase didn't want to see him get eaten by a gator either, but the result would probably be the same whether they moved him or not. He didn't think the levee road was going to be there tomorrow morning.

He took everything he thought he needed out of the pack, along with the satellite phone, and stuffed it all into his pockets, glad he had chosen to wear cargo pants that morning. He took a couple of pain pills and washed them down with water, which sent fire through his broken tooth. He cut a hole in the blanket for his head. Then he hung the GPS around his neck by its lanyard.

"Did you learn that from your dad?" Nicole asked.

"Funny," Chase said.

10:32 PM

Chase began to think they were walking backward instead of forward, or else that the GPS was wrong. How could it take over two hours to walk less than half a mile?

At this rate we won't get to the farm until sunrise, if at all!

The wind and rain were dissolving the road as if it were a sand castle. Twice they'd had to wade around a gap in waist-deep water. The last time, all three of them had nearly been swept out into the lake by the current rushing through the opening.

The ponchos, and the blanket he was wearing, were little help in this weather. Wet suits would have been better.

I'll have to suggest that to Dad, if I ever see him again, he thought. *And we need more batteries in the go bag too.*

He stopped to let everyone catch their breath and change the batteries in the headlamps, which were getting too dim to see.

"This is the last of the batteries. We're dead without light. We'll have to use one headlamp at a time. Whoever's wearing it will have to take the lead and call out problems to the two in back."

Whoever meant Chase or Nicole. Rashawn was doing a lot better than he expected, but every thirty minutes, like clockwork, she froze and burst into tears. The fits didn't last long, and she was perfectly fine when they were over, but he couldn't risk having her lead them up the dark road.

Nicole took the first lead, and it went smoothly for the first ten minutes, discounting the wind, the stinging rain, and Chase's throbbing front tooth, which the pain pills had done nothing to help.

Chase was a step behind Rashawn, holding on to her arm. Rashawn was a step behind Nicole, holding on to her arm. They'd tried hooking arms and walking three abreast, but when the crosswind gusted, it blew them into one another and their legs got tangled. The chain formation seemed to be working. When the wind picked one of them up off the road, which happened every few minutes, they would drop to their knees and huddle until it was safe to move again.

Huddle . . . hold . . . walk . . . Huddle . . . hold . . . walk . . .

"Stop!" Nicole shouted.

They huddled. Chase switched on his headlamp, expecting to see another breach in the road. But the road looked fine except for the large log up ahead. "We'll have to be careful," he said. "But we can get across that log."

Rashawn and Nicole laughed.

"What's so funny?"

"That ain't no log," Rashawn said. "That's a gator."

Chase stared ahead in horror. "That's not a gator, it's a *Tyrannosaurus rex*!"

"I thought you said the gators were riding out the storm underwater," Nicole said.

"Not this one. I bet he's thirteen feet if he's an inch. Probably fifty or sixty years old. My daddy would flip if he was here."

Chase wished her daddy was there to tell them what to do. The only way they could move forward was to scare it off the road or step over it.

"I'm surprised he hasn't moved, with the headlamp on him," Nicole said. "We must look like aliens to him."

"More like poachers," Rashawn said. "Which makes it even stranger he didn't bolt into the water as soon as he saw your light. They hunt them at night with spotlights. At his age and size I bet he has a bullet hole or two in him from poachers."

Chase looked at Nicole. "Any ideas?"

"I guess we move closer and see what the gator does."

11:02 PM

". . . as you can see, Richard . . . Emily has bypassed Saint Pete. All we have here is a bit of rain and some wind as the outer edge is skirting past us, heading north. It made landfall at 7:00 PM in Palm Breeze."

"Where I live," Richard said.

"I hope your family is safe, Richard."

"I hope so too. The last time I spoke to them, which was just after my wife got home from school — she's a principal, you know — everything was fine. An hour later I called back and the cell and landlines were completely dead.

"I guess what I don't understand — and I'm sure our viewers are wondering the same thing — is how could the forecasters be so wrong? Emily's landed fifty miles north of here. But what's even more surprising is that she made landfall four hours early, stranding

tens of thousands of people trying to get home or leave the area."

"Those are some pretty big questions, Richard. I hardly to know where to begin. . . .

"Everything we know about hurricanes is based on previous data. Emily is an anomaly. This afternoon she was moving faster than any other hurricane on record. No one could have predicted that she would actually pick up speed as the afternoon progressed. Because of her speed and her direction changes, forecasters were simply unable to predict where she would make landfall.

"As to the tens of thousands of stranded people, I don't think it's that many, but there are certainly people who have gotten caught by this storm. As you mentioned, Richard, we have a complete communications blackout with the exception of satellite phones. Here's what we think is going on, and please remember that none of this information can be verified until communications have been restored.

"All roads in and out of Palm Breeze have been closed due to flooding, wind damage, or car accidents. Because of the severe

weather, all nonessential emergency person-
nel have been sent home until such time that
the weather allows them to return.

"There have been seventeen reported
fatalities, and I want to emphasize that these
are reported, not verified. Five people have
died in automobile accidents, two people had
heart attacks, and three people have drowned.
The rest were reported killed by flying debris
and in building collapses.

"Law enforcement and emergency work-
ers have set up dozens of temporary shelters
in schools and other government buildings.
Those stranded in their cars have been moved
into the shelters to wait out the storm.

"There is no doubt that the area has
received a great deal of damage and there
will be more to come. I don't want to specu-
late any further."

"Do we have news crews headed up
there?"

"No, Richard. As I said, no one is being
allowed in or out, including local and national
news media. We've tried, but we were turned
back. Officials will reevaluate the situation in
the morning and let us know when we'll be
allowed in."

"As a resident with a family there, they would certainly allow me through."

"They are turning all residents away, Richard. The problem is the roads. They aren't passable. And with Emily in full swing, it's simply too dangerous."

"Thank you, Cindy. Right now we need to take a short commercial break. We'll be back with more about the storm of the century."

As soon as the camera stopped, Cindy shook her head in disgust and handed the mic to her young cameraman, Mark.

"Richard's a piece of work," Mark said.

"You got that right."

Cindy walked over to a 4x4 truck. John Masters was sitting in the cab with the door open, looking at a map on his laptop.

"Any luck?"

"Reaching Chase on the sat phone? No."

"Maybe his battery's dead."

"Chase makes sure all of our phones are charged. The sat phone is either broken or he's in trouble. He'd have the phone on by now if it worked. The school secretary called and said he'd been put on a bus. Hard to break a phone on a bus."

"Maybe they stopped the bus and moved him into a shelter."

"He'd still be able to call from the sat phone if it worked."

"From what you've told me, he knows how to take care of himself."

"He does. But I've got to make sure he's okay." John pointed to the map on the computer screen.

"You're going up there."

John nodded. He had been with Cindy on and off throughout the day. They'd had lunch and dinner together. They'd also been together when Chase called from school that afternoon.

"I have pretty good sources," Cindy said. "There is no way in or out of Palm Breeze, and it's going to stay that way until at least tomorrow, maybe longer."

"There is always a way in," John said.

"Devil's advocate," Cindy said. "Let's say you manage to get past all the roadblocks. Chase may not be at the farm."

"Wherever he is, we'll be closer," John said. "And I'll be where the damage is. There's not much to fix around here."

"What do you mean by *we'll*?"

"Tomás and I. We'll take different routes and keep in touch on the sat phones and CB. We'll get in. We've done it before." He looked at Cindy for a moment, considering. . . .

"What?" Cindy asked.

"Do you want to come with us?"

Cindy smiled and looked at her watch. "I'm off the clock until tomorrow morning. What are the chances of getting me back in time for work?"

"I would say the chances are absolutely zero."

"Fine, then I'm taking my work with me."

She looked over at Mark, who was packing his camera up. Cindy called him over.

"What's happening?"

"Do you want to head up north to the hurricane of the century with two complete strangers, without pay, without telling the station . . . oh, and you'll probably get fired if the hurricane doesn't kill you first?"

"Sounds good," Mark answered. "Let me get my camera."

11:09 PM

Chase, Nicole, and Rashawn were standing — crouching, actually, so they wouldn't get blown off the road — about thirty feet from the largest gator any of them had ever seen.

It looked a lot bigger than thirteen feet to Chase, and it hadn't moved an inch during their noisy approach. They had yelled, jumped up and down, and even thrown rocks at it. Chase was certain he'd hit the gator at least twice.

"You're the lion tamer," Chase said to Nicole. "What do we do?"

"I'm not a lion tamer," Nicole said. "And even if I was, there's a big difference between a lion and a gator."

"Yeah," Chase said. "About eight feet of difference." He looked at Rashawn. "What do you think?"

"I've seen a lot of gators, but I've never seen one act like this. Maybe he's dead. I'll tell you one thing: It wasn't easy for him to get up that slippery bank. Gators don't move so good uphill. Especially ones this size."

"Fate," Chase said.

"What?" Nicole and Rashawn said at the same time.

"Fate," Chase repeated. "I mean what are the chances of a

thirteen-foot gator hauling out onto this levee during a hurricane and dying lengthwise across the road at the very moment we need to walk past?"

"So, you're saying you don't think it's dead," Nicole said.

"I'm saying it doesn't make any difference. Dead or alive, we have to get by this prehistoric speed bump or we're going to die on this road. One way or the other we're dead."

He took the GPS from around his neck and slipped it over Nicole's head. Before they could say anything he half walked, half crawled toward the behemoth, angling toward its tail, thinking it would be easier to step over the tail than the body or snout. And the tail couldn't bite him.

But gator tails do move, Chase discovered, like armored whips. Just as he was stepping over, the tail came to life, flicking his feet out from under him. The gator's head whipped around and its jaws snapped closed loudly enough to be heard above the howling wind.

Chase dove headfirst over the bank and rolled, stopping just before he hit the water. He heard the gator following him over and began scrambling as fast as he could on his hands and knees along the water. He heard a splash behind him and immediately started crawling up the bank, hoping Rashawn was right about how difficult it was for a large gator to get up a slippery hill.

When he reached the road, he lay on his back, gasping. Nicole's and Rashawn's worried faces appeared above him. They pulled him to his feet and half dragged him fifty feet down the road before they had to stop to catch their breath.

"That might have been the stupidest thing I've ever seen a human do with a wild animal," Nicole said.

"It worked," Chase said, but he knew she was right. He'd have to rank it right up there with leaving the tools in the backyard so his father could get struck by lightning.

"We thought the gator ate you!" Nicole said.

"He wouldn't have eaten him," Rashawn said matter-of-factly. "At least not right away. He would have killed him and buried his body underwater in the mud, then waited for it to rot so he could tear off the soft flesh and gulp it down."

"Well, that's a relief," Nicole said.

She and Chase started laughing.

Rashawn smiled. "I'm not so sure what you two find so funny about alligator eating habits. Lying across the road playing possum is how that gator hunts." She pointed to the spot where the gator had been parked. "There's only one way across this water without swimming. When a deer, or some other kind of animal, comes along down the road, he just waits and snaps it up when it gets close enough. I bet that's how he got so big and old."

"And fast," Chase added. "I've never seen anything move like that."

"Speaking of which," Nicole interrupted, "we need to get moving."

Chase retrieved his GPS from Nicole's neck and turned it back on.

"A little over a mile and we're off the levee. Two miles after that, we're at your front gate."

01:15 AM

Every few hundred feet the levee was breached.

They made it across the first four gaps by climbing down in the gap and forming a human chain, linking hands so they weren't swept out into the lake by the water gushing through.

The fifth breach was three times wider than the others, and only twenty-five feet beyond the last one.

"We're on an island," Nicole said.

"A very tiny island," Rashawn confirmed.

Chase glanced back at the previous breach just in time to see a large piece of asphalt slough off. "And it just got smaller. The chain idea is not going to work here. It's too wide. We have to figure out an alternative."

If he ever saw his father again, he was going to suggest several new items for the go bag. Right now a length of rope would be pretty handy.

"I think I can jump it," Rashawn said.

Chase and Nicole stared at her. She was big and strong, but she didn't look like she could jump a fifteen-foot gap and land on a jagged piece of asphalt.

"What are you looking at?" Rashawn said. "You're not the only athlete here. I'm a good long jumper. The best at my old school. I got a case of medals and trophies to prove it."

"If you made it across," Nicole said. "How would that help *us*?"

"I'll scramble down, anchor myself on the other side, and hold out my free arm. I got a very long reach. We'll build a chain from the other side. Chase can grab my hand, you grab his, and I'll pull you both across."

"A running start is going to be nearly impossible with this crosswind," Chase pointed out.

"We have to do something," Rashawn said. "What have we got to lose?"

"You," Nicole said.

Chase glanced back again at the breach behind them. "Rashawn's right. If we don't do something right now, we'll end up in the lake."

Rashawn pulled her poncho off and handed it to Chase. "Stuff that into one of your Boy Scout pockets. It'll just get in my way. I'll need to have you stand on both sides of the road, shining both headlamps on my landing spot on the other side. I'll jump right between you."

Chase switched his headlamp on and took the right side. Nicole took the left, about fifteen feet away.

Rashawn walked back to the previous breach, checking for anything on the road that might trip her. She took a couple of deep breaths, stared at her landing spot on the other side, then took off.

Chase was right about the crosswind. He noticed Rashawn angling to his side, and he hoped it would be enough to compensate for the drift when she was in the air. He and Nicole stared in horror as Rashawn sailed off the edge, then stalled midway across as if she'd smashed into an invisible wall. She seemed to hover for a moment, her arms and legs flailing away as if she were trying to fly. Then she dropped like a stone into the black rushing water.

01:19 AM

"So, John Masters," Cindy said. "What do you really do for a living?"

"I'm just a working guy, traveling around helping people."

"I didn't ask what you did. I asked how you make a living."

"What's the difference?"

"Money, for one thing. It must cost a lot to travel around helping people. How do you pay for it?"

"Are you a meteorologist or a reporter?"

"Right now I'm a weather woman. In my previous life, which was about a year ago, I was an investigative journalist. A good one . . . too good, as it turned out. I was investigating a case of political corruption in San Francisco. Turns out that the man who owned the television station I worked for was up to his eyeballs in the scandal. And so was our lead news anchor, who also happened to be my now ex-husband, who happened to know a lot more about me than I wanted the public to know. Long story short. They won. I lost. And I got a job as far away as I could, hoping to get promoted to investigative journalist again."

"Is that why you don't like news anchors?"

"You mean Richard Krupp? I don't like Richard because he's an arrogant jerk. But he is the top-rated anchor in Saint Pete. The viewers adore him. And he hates me."

John laughed. "I can see why. I saw you throw him under the bus several times, and that's just when I was watching."

"Bad move on my part. By contract, Richard has final say on all on-camera promotions. I'm pretty certain I'll be looking for another job as soon as Emily blows herself out."

"Even though you were right about where Emily would make landfall," John said.

"I didn't know where she would land. I just reported that we didn't know. I'm kind of old-fashioned in that regard. Reporters should report what they know, not what they think or want to have happen. Just once in my life I'd like to see a reporter, or a talking head with a half-hour time slot to fill, say, 'Sorry, folks, we don't have any news worth reporting tonight. Instead we're going to run an episode of *SpongeBob SquarePants*. Check back with us tomorrow and we'll let you know if anything has changed.'"

John laughed. "That's never going to happen."

"You're right, and it's a shame."

"Why'd you hitch a ride with me?"

"If I recall — and I am a trained reporter — you asked if I wanted to go with *you*."

"I stand corrected," John said.

Cindy nodded. "I'll tell you why I accepted your offer. If you can get us through, I'll be able to get footage. That might save my job. It would also show up Richard Krupp. Like all good journalists, I'm very competitive. You can bet that Richard is in a news van right now with a producer, a cameraman, a sound person, and his makeup artist."

"I'm not here to get footage," John said. "I'm here to find Chase. Something's happened. I think he's in trouble."

"I understand. We won't get in your way, and I'll help any way I can, but I want to be honest. A father trying to save his son in a hurricane is a good story." John looked through the windshield at the rain. "Can we get back to the original subject?" Cindy asked.

"What's that?"

"You."

John pointed at the flashing red and blue lights beyond the windshield. "Let's wait and see if we can talk our way through this roadblock first. If you get past the first roadblock, the others are usually a breeze. And don't pull the TV card on them. They don't want you here. That's the best way to get turned around."

"Where's Tomás?"

"He's taking a road less traveled."

Cindy smiled, then recited:

> "I shall be telling this with a sigh
> Somewhere ages and ages hence:
> Two roads diverged in a wood, and I —
> I took the one less traveled by,
> And that has made all the difference."

"'The Road Not Taken' by Robert Frost," John said. "Tomás is a genius at finding back roads into towns. And perhaps more important, roads out of towns if we need to leave quickly because of a storm. But his routes are less direct and more dangerous."

"So, are you a man who takes the road less traveled?" Cindy asked.

"I'm just a working guy who travels roads."

"I don't believe you, John."

John looked through the wet windshield at the flashing police lights, then glanced back into the crew cab, where Mark was sound asleep.

"Cover that camera with a coat or something," he said. "If they see it, we're not going anywhere."

01:20AM

Nicole didn't hesitate. She dove over the edge immediately.

Chase dove in a split second later.

He was surprised by the power of the current. As he tumbled through the breach a large chunk of asphalt from the other side broke off and hit him in the right shoulder, pushing him under for a second or two. He surfaced, sputtering, shoulder aching, his arm going numb. He realized that even if Rashawn had made it across, the asphalt would have broken loose and she would have still ended up in the water.

He let the current carry him into deeper water where it was calmer. He was a good swimmer, but he had no doubt that Nicole was better. He looked around for her light and finally saw it fifty yards farther out, bobbing in the windblown whitecaps. That's when he remembered the gators. Thousands of them, Rashawn had said. But he was worried about one in particular. Where was that big boy now?

He swam forward, calling for Rashawn. It was difficult

going, with his sore shoulder and the stuff in his pockets weighing him down. He thought about dumping some of it but resisted the urge. Before the night was over they might need everything he was carrying.

He drew close enough to Nicole to hear her shouting for Rashawn.

He had no idea how good a swimmer Rashawn was. After all they'd been through, he did not want to lose her.

"Rashawn!" he shouted. "Rashawn!"

He reached Nicole. They were both exhausted and out of breath.

"No sign of her?"

"None. Rashawn!"

"What do you want to do?" Chase asked.

Nicole didn't answer him. "Rashawn! Swim toward the light. Shout! We'll swim to you!"

They listened. All they heard was the wind. All they saw was a lake that looked like a stormy sea.

"How far are we from the levee?" Nicole asked.

"Farther than we should be."

Nicole looked at her watch. "Ten minutes! You swim that way, I'll swim this way."

Chase shook his head. "I'll swim for five minutes, then I'm going to swim toward shore. This will give me time to get in front of the breach. That way you'll know where to swim to. We don't want to go through this a second time. When you come in, swim toward my light. If you find her or you need help, hit the button on the headlamp twice. That will send it into emergency blinking mode with alternating white and red lights. I'll do the same if I find her or need help. Good luck."

"You too," Nicole responded. "We're gonna need it."

01:23 AM

"What are you doing out here?" the sopping-wet policeman shouted through the driver's window of John's truck.

"Emergency services," John answered calmly.

The policeman acted like he hadn't heard him. "Maybe you missed the memo, or maybe you're just insane. Do you realize that you're driving around in a Category Five hurricane?"

The shouting policeman woke Mark. He pushed his long hair behind his ears. "What's happening?"

Cindy turned. "Go back to sleep."

"Fat chance. Where are we?"

The policeman shined his light in Mark's face. "You're smack-dab in the middle of the biggest hurricane ever to hit here. Maybe the biggest to hit the United States."

"I heard that it's been downgraded to a Category Four," John said.

"Three, four, five . . . makes no difference to me. It's destroyed every road up ahead. It's an ongoing disaster. A national disaster."

"Which is why we're here," John said. "We're contractors. If the roads are impassable ahead, how did you get here?"

The policeman glared at him for a second, then said, "I just turned back two Federal Emergency Management Agency trucks. The FEMA people weren't too happy with me either, but I have my orders. The only people we're letting through are law enforcement and National Guard. We'll let you know when you can pass."

"It's hard to help people if you aren't there to help them," John said.

"I hear you, but there's nothing I can do. And there's nothing you can do for anybody in a little four-by-four with a winch."

"We have two big rigs stationed ahead with supplies." Cindy raised her eyebrows but didn't contradict him.

"Providing that your rigs are still intact, and there's a good chance they aren't. As bad as it is here, it's worse up ahead. A lot worse. About five miles back down the road is a high school. We've set up a temporary shelter in the gym. You'll find uncomfortable cots, bad coffee, stale donuts, and dozens of annoyed people just like you waiting to get through to do their thing. Don't expect to get through until midmorning at the earliest. We'll assess the damage and let you know if and when you can proceed."

John turned the truck around and headed back down the road.

"It's not that long before daylight," Mark said. "Bet that shelter is filled with news people. I'm kind of partial to bad coffee and day-old donuts."

John passed his Thermos back to him. "Help yourself. There's half a box of donuts under the seat. You'll need the bad coffee to soften them up."

Mark took the Thermos. "I take that to mean that we're not going to the shelter."

"Nope."

"Then where are we going?"

"The road less traveled," Cindy said.

"First I have to talk to Tomás."

John pulled to the side of the road and called his partner on his sat phone. They proceeded to have a short conversation in Spanglish, which Cindy and Mark could barely understand. He ended the call and punched in some coordinates on his in-dash GPS, then studied the map.

"Tomás thinks he's found a way past the roadblock. Do either of you know how to use a chain saw?"

01:28AM

Chase swam in widening circles for six minutes, shouting Rashawn's name, listening, then shouting again, ignoring the pain in his shoulder. He hated to stop looking, but they had to get back to shore or risk drowning themselves. He treaded water and looked at his GPS. Rather than risk having to cross another breach he decided he'd haul out where the road ended. As he swam toward shore he continued to call out for Rashawn.

Nicole was exhausted and hoarse from shouting.
Rashawn wouldn't be able to hear me from twenty feet away.
She spotted Chase's light, which seemed impossibly far away in the dark rough water.
"Rashawn! Rashawn!"

Chase stumbled up on shore, staying low to the ground to keep from getting knocked over by the wind. He shined his headlamp all around, looking for gators, then sat down on the bank to catch his breath.

Now that he was still he could feel the throbbing pain in his shoulder. If he had jumped a second later, the entire slab of asphalt might have hit him, knocking him out, or worse, pinning him underwater.

He scanned the churning water for Nicole's light and began to panic when he didn't see it. He stood and squinted against the rain, then let out a sigh of relief when he spotted a pinpoint of light much farther away than it should have been.

If she's having trouble, the light should be flashing. What is she doing?

"Thank God you're okay!"

Chase nearly pitched forward into the water. "Rashawn? What are you doing here?"

She ran forward and threw her big arms around him, crunching his shoulder, but he was so happy to see her he didn't care. She squeezed him tighter and he grunted in pain.

She let go of him. "You hurt? What's the matter?"

"Some of the road fell on me when we went in after you, but I'm fine. What happened to you?"

"I really thought I could make it across, but you were right about the wind. It picked me up like I was a goose feather, then the current sucked me under. I thought for sure I was going to drown. When I finally came up I had no idea where I was. I just started swimming and climbed out about a hundred yards down from here. I hurried back to the breach, which is huge now. When I didn't see you or Nicole, I freaked. I thought you got washed away. Where were you?"

"We jumped in the water after you. We kept calling, but you couldn't hear us up on the road."

"Where's Nicole?"

Chase pointed to the water.

"You mean that tiny light out there?"

"She should be heading in by now, but it doesn't look like she's getting any closer. I'm worried. She's been out there too long."

"This is all my fault," Rashawn sobbed. "If I hadn't tried to jump, you and —"

Chase cut her off. "If you hadn't tried to jump, one or all of us might have been crushed by the asphalt that got me. We were wasting time talking. You got us moving."

"Thanks, Chase."

"It's the truth."

"Let's get Nicole." She started toward the water.

Chase took her arm and pulled her back. "I'm not going to get far with this bum shoulder. And I'm not about to let you get back in the water. We need to stick together. I'll let her know you're safe. Let's get up on the road."

They scrambled to the top. It was hard to believe, but the wind seemed to be blowing even harder. They had to get on their knees and hang on to each other to keep from being blown back over the edge into the water.

Chase took his headlamp off, switched it to emergency mode, and held it above his head. He hoped Nicole could see the light. He hoped she'd understand that Rashawn was with him. He hoped she had the stamina to make it back to shore against the wind.

01:41AM

Everything the makeup artist had done to Richard Krupp's face and hair came undone the moment he stepped outside into Emily. The sound and ferocity of the wind and rain scared him and his two-man crew half to death. If the crew hadn't been there, Richard might have run back through the doorway they'd just slipped through. He locked arms with his cameraman, who in turn linked up with the sound guy. The three of them made their way to the filming location they'd picked from the van when they first drove up. When they'd chosen the spot, it had looked easy to get to. Halfway there, they all had serious doubts. Bits of flying debris slammed into their Gore-Tex rain suits like shotgun pellets.

"We should be wearing body armor!" the cameraman shouted.

"I'm getting way too old for this . . ." The sound guy's last word was carried away by the wind.

Richard was speechless. It was all he could do to move his legs forward and breathe. The wind was blowing so hard it was tough to catch enough to fill his lungs.

He was worried about getting hit by a large chunk of debris. He was also worried about being completely blown away by the wind. But his biggest concern was how he was going to look on camera and what he was going to say.

If they could manage to get the video uploaded, there was a good chance that it would be played all over the world. His producer wanted to run a live feed of the video, but Richard insisted on a review before it hit the airwaves. He argued that at this time of morning, viewership would be low, especially locally with the widespread power outages. He wanted a second shot if he didn't like the first one. But now that he was out in the storm, he had absolutely no desire for a second take. Somehow he had to mask his abject terror with a look of calm courage.

The cameraman stopped, and started pushing buttons on the video camera and wiping the lens. "You're going to have to do double duty!" he shouted at the sound guy. "You'll have to keep the lens dry!"

"Can't you just change the angle?" his coworker shouted back. "I'm going to have my hands full with the sound in this wind."

"It doesn't matter what angle the camera is at. The rain's coming from every direction. The lens is going to get drenched."

The sound guy looked at Richard. "You'll have to use the hardwire mic. The wind's too loud for the lapel or boom mic." He handed the mic to Richard. "Hold it right to your lips. Don't shout, but talk loud, or no one's going to hear you. On three."

Richard spread his legs and braced himself as best as he could. He tried to set his expression into "bravery in the grip of terrible adversity" but it was difficult with the wind contorting his face as if he were in a free fall without a parachute.

The cameraman held up his index finger. When his ring finger went up, Richard began.

"If Emily has been downgraded to a Category Four hurricane, I would hate to be standing in a Category Five hurricane to bring you this update.

"As you can see, I'm right in the thick of it. All around me is complete and utter devastation as I try to get home to my loved ones. But they say there is no way home. Every road in is impassable. I've fought my way through the storm all night, and I'll continue to fight regardless of personal risk.

"I realize that it's difficult for you watching in your living rooms to get a true sense of Emily's power, but let me tell you ... it ... is ... immense. I have stood in the face of at least a dozen hurricanes in my life, but never one of this magnitude.

"I'm going to sign off now because I need to push forward. Stay tuned and stay safe. I'll update you when I can."

Richard stared at the camera for a dramatic beat, then gave the crew a nod to shut the equipment down. "Let's get out of here."

Huddled together against the wind and rain, they shuffled fifteen feet to their left, yanked open a door, and stumbled into a large gymnasium filled with people, cots, food, water, warmth, light, the smell of coffee, and the hum of generators.

His producer met them with an armload of fluffy white towels, hot coffee, and a dozen glazed donuts.

Richard grabbed a towel and looked down at the box of donuts. "No sugar donuts?"

"They're out," the producer said. "But the rumor is that more are on the way. How'd the shoot go?"

"We'll have to run tape to be sure, but I think it's good."

"You weren't out there very long."

"And you weren't out there at all," Richard snapped. "I just risked my life." He grabbed two donuts. "Let's take a look at the vid and get it on the air. I need to get some sleep."

01:53 AM

John, Cindy, and Mark had left the main road and managed to circumvent the first roadblock.

John bumped the 4x4 back onto the highway and stepped on the gas. He'd been on the sat phone with Tomás almost constantly.

"Tomás says they aren't letting anyone past the roadblock he's at, but he thinks he's found a way around it. He's waiting for us seven miles up ahead. If we can get around it, we're home free." A large branch hit the windshield and cracked it. "Well, at least we'll be past the authorities. We'll still have to deal with Emily."

Cindy looked at her watch. "That should just about give you enough time to tell me about your earring."

John stared straight ahead, then told her what it felt like to get struck by lightning.

01:54 AM

"I think her light is definitely getting bigger," Rashawn said.

Chase couldn't tell, but he was certain the wind was blowing harder. He and Rashawn were nearly hugging the road, trying to stay in one place. He hoped that when Nicole made it to shore she had enough strength left in her legs to walk.

"Maybe I should swim out to her," Rashawn suggested again.

"I thought you said she was getting closer."

"I think she is. But she's been in the water a long time. She has to be getting tired."

"Let's wait," Chase said, but he was tempted to let Rashawn go. The problem was that they might have to carry Nicole, and he would need Rashawn to help him. They were fifty yards from the end of the levee road. As soon as Nicole reached shore they'd have to move quickly or they'd be back in the water with the gators. According to the GPS, about a hundred yards past the levee the road took a sharp turn to the left. If the wind held its current direction, it would be at their backs all the way to the road the Rossi farm was on. Two miles up that road was the gate. They were less than three miles from safety.

"Three miles!" he said aloud, but the words were swept away by Emily.

"I'm so sorry about your wife and little girl. I don't know how I would have —"

Something large and loud slammed into the side of the truck. John yanked the steering wheel toward the impact and stepped on the gas, trying to get the 4x4 under control. The truck slid sideways for twenty feet, then came to an abrupt stop against something hard.

The air bags deployed.

The engine stopped.

John felt the side of his head where it had bounced off the window. There was a bump the size of an egg, but no blood.

"Everyone okay?" he asked, pushing the air bag away from his face.

"You need side-impact air bags."

"I'll get them when I replace this truck, which I probably just totaled."

"There are *no* air bags back here," Mark said. "But I'm fine even though we just got hit by a flying tree."

"We got hit by a boulder," John said. "Then we hit a tree."

"Whatever," Mark said.

Bright headlights filled the windshield.

"Tomás," John said. They'd been following him on back roads for nearly fifteen minutes.

John tried to start the engine.

"Dead." He rolled the window down.

A yellow rain slicker appeared at the window. "Hurt?"

"No, but I think we're going to have to buy another truck. Let's get the stuff transferred."

Tomás nodded, then jogged around the back, seemingly oblivious to Emily's fury. A few minutes later they were back on the road, with Tomás behind the wheel and Saint Christopher on the dash.

02:11 AM

Nicole knew she should have headed back to shore sooner, but every time she started in that direction the possibility of missing Rashawn's call for help stopped her. Finally she saw Chase's red and white flashing light. It was above her, which meant it had to be up on the road. Chase was either in trouble, or Rashawn was with him. She prayed it was the latter and started toward the light.

It turned out to be the most difficult thing she'd ever done in her life. She was swimming hard, but Chase's light was not getting closer. In fact, it looked like it was getting farther away. And it was. Despite her efforts, the wind was pushing her backward. She began to think she should turn around and swim to the opposite shore, but she had no idea how far away it was, or how hard it would be to get back around to the levee. The lake was surrounded by thick vegetation. She might have to find a place to shelter and wait out the storm.

She decided to try to reach Chase one more time before giving herself to the wind.

* . * *

"See?" Rashawn shouted.

Chase squinted against the rain at Nicole's light.

"It's getting bigger!" Rashawn said. "And there's a pattern to it. Her light disappears at regular intervals. The whitecaps could not possibly be causing that."

Nicole's headlamp did seem to be getting bigger, or at least brighter. Chase stared at it until it disappeared. He glanced at his watch, noted the second, then looked back at the water where the light had been. The light reappeared. He looked at his watch. Thirty seconds. The light bobbed crazily for ten seconds, then disappeared again. He timed it two more intervals. They were the same within a couple of seconds. He looked at Rashawn.

"See what I mean?" she said.

What Chase saw was a sixth-grade girl with incredible courage. Instead of succumbing to paralyzing fear, like any normal person would in a storm like this, she'd been able to figure out the pattern to Nicole's swimming. This meant that Rashawn was no longer afraid.

Fear extinguishes thought.

In the past year, not a week had gone by without his father reminding him of this.

Rashawn had just reminded him again.

02:15 AM

Tomás slowed the truck and came to a stop a few feet in front of a downed tree blocking the road.

"Guess it's time to see how a chain saw works in hundred-and-fifty-mile-an-hour winds," John said.

Tomás was out of the truck before John finished the sentence. John turned to Cindy and Mark.

"Stay put," he said.

"No way," Cindy said. "We need to start getting some footage for *The Man Who Got Struck by Lightning*."

"Huh?"

"The documentary I'm planning to produce about you."

"I'm not sure I like the name, or being filmed," John said.

"We can discuss the title later," Cindy said. "Grab your camera, Mark."

Tomás's yellow form appeared in front of the headlights, holding a chain saw. He fired the saw up, but the sound was overwhelmed by the wind.

John jumped out and joined him. Tomás had brought two chain saws, but they immediately decided it would be safer for one of them to use the saw while the other pulled branches and pieces of trunk out of the way.

"Try not to get blown away," Cindy said to Mark. "And don't think news segment. Think documentary. This is not a whoa-look-at-me-I'm-in-a-hurricane-and-I-can-barely-stand-up thing. This is the real deal."

"*The Man Who Got Struck By Lightning* thing," Mark said.

"That's right." Cindy had trouble opening the crew-cab door because of the wind. She finally resorted to pushing it open with her feet. She had to hold on to the door handles, then the front wheel well, to keep from getting blown away. Mark had reached the front of the truck and was already filming by the time she got there. He was holding on to the winch with one hand and the camera with the other.

John had been in a lot of storms, but nothing like this. The branches lashed their heads, arms, backs, and legs like bullwhips. There was hardly any need to haul anything away. As soon as Tomás cut through something, it blew off into the darkness.

All John could really do to help him was to shout out when a piece of flying debris was coming his way.

He glanced behind him and saw the camera light. Cindy started to crawl forward, but he waved her back with both hands. They didn't need her help. Tomás barely needed *his* help.

02:20AM

When Nicole got about fifty feet from shore, Chase and Rashawn slid down the muddy embankment. Chase waved his flashing headlamp over his head. Rashawn cheered Nicole on as if she were competing in the Olympics. At twenty feet they both waded into the water, grabbed Nicole under her arms, and dragged her to shore. Chase gently removed her headlamp and handed it to Rashawn. Minutes passed before Nicole, was even able to speak.

She looked up at Rashawn. "I'm so happy you're okay. I thought you drowned."

"I thought you were going to drown trying to save me!" Rashawn started crying.

Nicole took her hand and started crying too.

Chase looked at his watch. He gave them about half a minute, then said, "We have to get off the levee before it collapses. Can you walk?"

Nicole sat up slowly. "I'm not sure. My arms and legs feel like noodles."

"Let her rest some more," Rashawn said.

Chase nodded, but he really wanted to get moving. "Rashawn noticed that your light kept disappearing."

Nicole smiled. "I was getting pushed to the other side of the lake by the wind. The only way to get around it was to avoid it. I started to think about what Rashawn had said about the gators sitting on the bottom riding out the storm. I dove and swam underwater and under the wind. I lost ground every time I came up for air, but not as much as I was gaining. I don't think I would have made it if I'd waited five minutes more figuring this out."

Nicole turned her head and looked at the steep bank. "I'm not sure I can make it up to the road."

"We'll help you," Chase said. He and Rashawn got on either side and pulled her onto her feet.

Nicole tried to stand on her own and would have fallen over if they hadn't caught her.

"We can carry you," Rashawn said.

"Not up that, you can't."

"We'll get you up there even if we have to drag you," Chase said. "But the wind's a lot stronger up on the road."

"My legs will come back," Nicole said. "They always have before. How far is it to the farm?"

"After we get off the levee, a couple of miles."

"My legs feel better already," Nicole said.

Chase draped Nicole's arm around his neck. Rashawn did the same with Nicole's other arm.

On the first attempt they made it halfway up the bank,

then stumbled, and all three of them slid back down to the water. The second try wasn't much better. On the third they were within inches of the top when Nicole's legs went completely dead. She reeled over backward, taking Chase and Rashawn with her.

"Just leave me here!" Nicole said. "You and Rashawn go to the farm and get my dad!"

"Forget it," Chase said. "We're sticking together."

Rashawn started massaging Nicole's legs.

"That hurts!"

"Good," Rashawn said. "It's supposed to hurt. Some athlete you are. I gotta get the circulation going in your limbs. Push out all that nasty lactic acid poisoning your muscles."

Nicole knew all about lactic acid buildup, but she was surprised Rashawn knew about it, and what to do to get rid of it. After a long or fast swim the team's physical therapist always gave her a rubdown.

"How do you know about lactic acid?"

"I told you, you aren't the only athlete here."

"We really have to go," Chase said.

"We aren't going anywhere until we get some life back into these legs," Rashawn snapped. "If we'd done this in the first place, we'd be off the levee by now."

"Rashawn's right," Nicole said.

Chase nodded, then looked at Rashawn. "I'll work on one leg, you work on the other."

02:35AM

Tomás and John climbed back into the truck after cutting through their third tree. Cindy and Mark had stayed in the cab because getting in and out wasted too much time.

"That should be the last one for a while," John said, wiping his head with an already sopping towel. "There's a lake up ahead."

Tomás put the truck into gear and stepped on the accelerator. The wipers could barely keep up with the rain, and the defroster was having a hard time with the damp heat coming off their bodies, making it nearly impossible for them to see through the windshield.

As soon as they left the tree cover, they were hit by a vicious blast of wind. The truck fishtailed, but Tomás got it under control and pushed ahead. The sheeting rain prevented Cindy from seeing anything out her little side window.

Tomás slammed on the brakes and shouted something in Spanish that Cindy didn't understand. John began swearing. She understood everything he said.

Tomás put the truck into reverse and backed up twice as fast as they had driven forward.

"What's going on?" Mark shouted.

"Road's out," John said.

Tomás drove the truck back into the cover of the trees and stopped. He and John had another short conversation in Spanglish.

"We're going to walk back up and take a closer look at the levee road," John translated. "If we can't get across, we're going to have to backtrack all the way to where we met up with Tomás and find another way around."

"I'm going with you," Cindy said.

"No," John said. "The little bit of road we're on might collapse."

Cindy zipped her coat and pulled up her hood. Mark did the same.

"Suit yourself," John said.

They got out of the truck. John linked arms with Cindy. Tomás linked arms with Mark. In their free hands they carried heavy-duty flashlights.

They hunched into the powerful wind and shuffled forward. It took them several minutes to reach the break. It was twenty-five feet across, if not more.

John and Tomás got down on their stomachs and crawled to the very edge of the break. They shined their lights under the jagged asphalt and stuck their heads over the edge.

Cindy could not even imagine what they were looking for. It was a dead end. Getting across was impossible.

She looked down the long road and thought she saw something. She wiped the rain from her eyes and looked again.

"John!"

John got up.

"I saw a light. Maybe two lights."

"The power's out and we're in the middle of a refuge. No one lives here, which is one of the reasons we came this way. The road to the farm is on the other side of this lake."

"I saw it too," Mark said. "The light was a long way off, but I might have caught it on video."

"Where?" John asked.

Cindy pointed. "Straight down the road."

John held his light above his head and flashed it on and off several times. No lights flashed back at them.

"Let's get back to the truck," John said. "I'm not sure how long it's going to take to get around this lake. Or if there even is a way around it."

Tomás jockeyed the truck around and headed back the way they had come.

Cindy tapped John on the shoulder. "What were you and Tomás looking for over the edge of that road? For a second I thought you were trying to figure out a way of jumping it."

John laughed. "We hate backtracking, but we're not crazy . . . well, not that crazy. We were looking at how a levee disintegrates. It's not often that you get to see something like that. It's interesting."

"I've got news for you, John," Cindy said. "You *are* crazy."

"Nah, we're storm runners."

"Got it!" Mark said.

"What?"

"The lights. And Cindy was right, there were two of them."

Mark turned the camera around so they could see the small screen, and hit play. It wasn't very clear, but two lights definitely appeared at the end of the dark road. They moved from left to right, then disappeared.

"Play it back," John said.

Mark played it back in slow motion.

"That's pretty strange," John said. "I guess I should have been looking down the road instead of under it."

"What do you think they were?" Cindy asked.

John shook his head. "I have no idea, but weird phenomena happen during storms like this. Most of the time nobody sees them because we're inside under shelter."

"Maybe it was a couple of storm runners out for a stroll," Cindy said.

"Back the truck up!" John shouted.

Tomás immediately put it into reverse.

"What are you doing?" Cindy asked.

"I need to check something out. This is far enough."

Tomás slammed on the brakes, and John jumped out of the cab with his flashlight and began searching the road. Five minutes later he climbed back into the cab and grabbed his sat phone from the dash.

"What did you find?" Cindy asked.

"Tire tracks. School bus tire tracks. Those lights might have been Chase."

He punched in Chase's number.

03:00 AM

Rashawn's massage coupled with Nicole's determination to get home brought Nicole's legs back to life. They reached the road on the fourth try with relative ease. Once there, they didn't hesitate. They locked arms, with Nicole in the middle, and started walking, which got a lot easier when they turned to the left and had the wind at their backs. The only things they had to contend with were downed trees and flying debris. They stumbled out onto Nicole's road, bruised, cut, scraped, and out of breath, but they were alive, for which they were all very grateful.

Chase looked at his GPS while they took a short rest. He wasn't sure which part of his body hurt the most. His shoulder and tooth seemed to be in a sharp competition for the top spot.

"Half a mile to the gate," he said, covering his broken tooth with his upper lip so the wind couldn't get at it.

"There's a lot of water on the road," Nicole said.

Chase had been wet for so long he'd hardly noticed, but she was right. The water was up to their ankles. He tried to picture the long driveway up to the Rossi house and thought it was uphill, but he wasn't sure. He was so exhausted he was having a hard time focusing. The only things keeping him going were Nicole, who had to be more exhausted than he was, and Rashawn, who had turned out to be a bulldozer of will and endurance.

"Ready?" Rashawn said.

Chase nodded and was about to forge ahead when he felt something tickle his leg. He reached down to itch it and realized what it was.

"Wait!"

He pulled the sat phone out of his pocket and took it out of the plastic bag.

"Hello?"

"Where are you?" His father's voice sounded a million miles away.

"About a half a mile from the farm," Chase shouted above the wind. "The bus sank."

"Are you okay?"

"Yeah."

"Is the bus driver with you?"

"He's dead. I'm with Nicole Rossi and a girl named Rashawn. Where are you?"

"On the other side . . ."

"What?"

"We're . . . lake . . . saw . . . light . . ."

"Is that your father?" Nicole asked. "What's he saying?"

"Hang on," Chase said. He squatted down and pulled the blanket over his head to get the phone out of the wind and rain.

"Are . . . Chase?"

"I'm here, but you're breaking up."

"Get to . . . We'll be . . . as soon as . . ."

The phone went dead.

Chase put the phone back in the plastic bag and came out from under his makeshift shelter.

"That was my father," he reported to Nicole and Rashawn. "It was a lousy connection, but I think he's on the other side of the lake. He may have seen our headlamps on the other end of the levee. He's going to try to get to the farm. That's all I can tell you."

"So that phone of yours works?" Rashawn said.

Chase shook his head. "It worked for about twenty seconds, then it went out. If I can get it dried out, it might come back on. Let's go."

They locked arms and started up the road, with Nicole back in the middle, but this time they weren't holding Nicole up, they were holding one another up. None of them could have made it without the others.

As he leaned into the final stretch with his friends, Chase couldn't help but think about how the night would have gone if Dr. Krupp had listened to him.

They'd be in the cafetorium in the dark with the wind roaring outside, but safe, uninjured, with their bellies full from raiding the coolers and vending machines.

The bus driver would be alive at home with his family, if he had a family. Chase didn't even know the bus driver's name.

And what about his father and Tomás? Chase was certain his father was worried about him, but there was nothing he could do until the storm passed.

Save yourself. You're no good to anybody if you're dead . . . including yourself.

03:33 AM

At last they were standing at the gate, almost exactly twelve hours after they'd left the school.

"It's locked," Nicole said, obviously upset.

"Don't you have a key?" Chase asked.

"Of course, but that's not the problem. The padlock is hanging on the outside. We only lock the gate when we're not here. That means Dad isn't here. He must have gone out looking for us."

"What about Momma Rossi?" Chase asked.

"She would have stayed behind in case the phones came back on and I called."

"I'm sure your dad's fine. He probably got forced into a shelter."

"I hope so."

"Do you have a backup generator on the farm?"

"A small one, but it only powers one building at a time."

"We have three generators in the rigs. Let's get through and power the farm up."

Nicole unlocked the gate. They walked through. She closed the gate but didn't lock it.

The quad was exactly where Chase had parked it, though it had tipped over.

"Do you want to walk or try to ride up to the house?"

"Ride," Nicole and Rashawn said together.

"That's what I thought," Chase said. "But the quad is going to be unstable in the wind with three people on it. We'll have to keep a low profile. If it starts to tip, just lean the opposite way. No sudden moves. We don't want to flip it."

They righted the quad. Chase swung on first, turned the key, then pushed the ignition switch. It didn't start. With the rain and being tipped over by the wind, it could have any number of problems — none of which he could repair where they were. He adjusted the choke and pushed the ignition switch again.

"We might be walking after all." He made another adjustment to the choke, then let it set for a minute before giving the switch one last try.

It started . . . at least Chase thought it started. The quad was loud, but he couldn't hear the roar of the engine above the wind.

"Do you see the helmets anywhere?" He had left them hanging on the handlebars.

"They're long gone," Nicole said.

Chase laughed at himself. They had just spent half the night walking through a hurricane and he was worrying about helmets.

He pulled his headlamp off, handed it to Nicole. He told her to climb on behind him, and Rashawn to climb on behind Nicole.

"Everyone lean forward," he shouted. "Face your headlamps to the side in opposite directions and keep your eyes open. This way we'll have a hundred-and-eighty-degree view. If you see a problem, like a big branch flying in our direction, tap me on the shoulder in the direction it's coming. I'm going to drive directly to the farmhouse to check on Momma Rossi."

He leaned forward until his chin was almost touching his knees. Nicole draped herself over his back. Under other circumstances he might have felt very different about having Nicole this close to him, and he wondered if Nicole was thinking the same thing.

He started out slowly, getting a feel for the overloaded quad. The steering was sluggish in the crosswind.

Up ahead he remembered the road veering to the left. The wind would be at their backs and he might be able to pick up speed. There was standing water on the gravel road, but not nearly as much as there had been on the highway. The quad's balloon tires cut through the water easily, but he'd have to watch out for hydroplaning, which was just as dangerous as driving on ice.

He followed the road to the left and the steering became more responsive. He increased the speed, and tried to recall if there were any other turns before they reached the buildings below the house.

He felt a tap on his right shoulder and grimaced in pain. He looked to his right, but didn't see anything. He eased off the throttle, and something very strange happened.

The wind died and the rain stopped.

Completely.

Chase shut the quad off.

It was silent except for their breathing, which they hadn't been able to hear for hours.

Chase looked up and saw stars against a black sky.

"Weird," Rashawn said.

"The eye of the storm," Chase said. "It's going to start up again, and the back end of the hurricane might be worse than the front. Do you realize that we're talking in normal voices and not shouting at each other?"

"This eye-of-the-storm thing is not why I tapped you on the shoulder," Rashawn said.

"Then why?"

"I know you'll think I'm crazy. Maybe I dozed off, or maybe I'm so worn out I'm hallucinating, but I think I saw a big spotted cat running along my side. Looked like a leopard."

Chase and Nicole stared at her, absolutely speechless.

"I told you, you'd think I was crazy. But it gets stranger. The cat was carrying what looked like a little monkey in its mouth. The monkey was limp. It looked dead."

"Poco," Nicole said.

"Hector," Chase said.

"Are you saying I did see a leopard carrying a little green monkey? What kind of a farm is this?"

"Right now, a very dangerous farm," Nicole said.

Chase started the quad, put it into gear, and pushed the throttle as far as it would go. As they sped up the road he wondered how fast a leopard could run.

03:42 AM

Chase pulled up in front of the Rossis' house, or at least where it used to be. The old farmhouse looked like it had been pushed over by a bulldozer. Nicole was off the quad, screaming for Momma Rossi, before the quad came to a complete stop.

"This was their house?" Rashawn asked in shock.

"Yeah." Chase swung off the quad and stepped into a foot of water. "Can I borrow your headlamp?" Rashawn slipped it off her forehead. "You want to stay here with the quad while I get Nicole?"

"With a leopard running around?" Rashawn said. "No, thanks."

"That's why I have to get Nicole. We can't be standing out here in the open like this with Hector running around. And this eye isn't going to last long. When the wind starts up again, this debris is going to be blowing all over the place. We have to find shelter."

"Then let's get her and get out of here," Rashawn said.

Nicole was yelling for Momma Rossi and frantically pulling up floating debris. Chase put his hand on her shoulder.

"We need to go," he said gently.

"We need to find Momma Rossi!" Nicole shouted.

"She may not be here," Chase said. "I saw a light on outside one of the buildings."

Nicole turned around and looked. "The circus barn!"

She ran back to the quad, with Chase and Rashawn right behind her. When they reached the barn, Nicole was off the quad again before it stopped, and running to a side door.

"A lot of water here," Rashawn said as they hurried to the entrance.

"I know," Chase said.

Inside, Nicole had her arms wrapped around Momma Rossi. They were both crying. Chase was relieved Momma Rossi had made it through the storm, but he knew they were still far from safe. Three feet in from the door, there was a good six inches of standing water.

"Is that an elephant?" Rashawn asked.

"Her name's Pet," Chase said.

"Nicole's mom is kind of small."

"Don't let that fool you," Chase said. "She's bigger than she looks. And older — she's actually Nicole's grandmother."

They walked over, and Momma Rossi hugged them both.

"Where's Dad?" Nicole asked.

Momma Rossi shook her head. "I don't know. He left hours ago to see if he could find you. I was sitting in the house, waiting for you, when it started to come apart. I ran down here and I've been sitting here ever since. Did you stop at the house?"

Nicole nodded, tears rolling down her cheeks. "It's gone," she said quietly.

Momma Rossi put her arms around her. "It's just a house. We can rebuild a house. Did you see Poco up there? He jumped out of my arms and disappeared into the night."

Rashawn was about to say something, but Nicole cut her off. "We didn't see him," she said. "I'm sure he's fine."

"I'm sure your father's fine too," Momma Rossi said. "He'll be back now that the storm's over."

"It's not over," Chase said. "We're in the eye of —"

His words were cut off by a gust of wind slamming into the metal building. Pet pulled on her chains and threw hay and sawdust over her back with her gray trunk.

"That wind's going to scare the baby right out of her," Momma Rossi shouted above the noise.

Chase glanced again at the door. The water was rising.

STORM RUNNERS

Chase and his friends may have survived the worst of Hurricane Emily, but their troubles are just beginning.

Have they lived through a terrifying night only to face a new danger?

FIND OUT IN:

THE SURGE

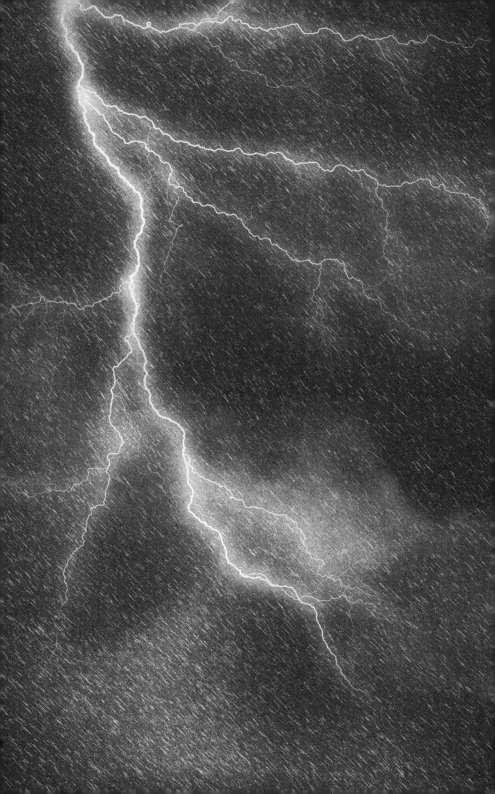

ABOUT THE AUTHOR

Roland Smith is the author of numerous award-winning books for young readers, including *Zach's Lie*, *Jack's Run*, *Cryptid Hunters*, *Peak*, *I, Q*, and, most recently, *Tentacles*. For more than twenty years, he worked as an animal keeper, traveling all over the world, before turning to writing full-time. Roland lives with his wife, Marie, on a small farm south of Portland, Oregon. Visit him online at www.rolandsmith.com.

TENTACLES

THE THRILLING SEQUEL TO CRYPTID HUNTERS BY
ROLAND SMITH

TROUBLED WATERS!

Cryptids — mythological creatures like the Loch Ness monster and Sasquatch — are Travis Wolfe's obsession, and he'll travel to the ends of the earth for proof. For cousins Marty and Grace, who have lived with Wolfe ever since Marty's parents disappeared, this means adventure — and danger! Now they're all en route to the South Pacific to track down a giant squid, but the freighter they're on seems to be haunted, and someone on board is determined to sabotage their mission. Will Marty and Grace get to the bottom of this fishy business — or end up at the bottom of the sea?

PRAISE FOR TENTACLES

"A high-octane page-turner that will reel readers in and keep them riveted."
— *School Library Journal*

"Smith's fast-paced story will capture the imagination of any action-loving reader."
— *BookPage*